A Slave to Magic

Tales from Nōl'Deron

Lana Axe

AxeLord Publications
ISBN-10: 0692405232
ISBN-13: 978-0692405239

Cover art by Michael Gauss

The moment the slave resolves that he will no longer be a slave,
his fetters fall.
He frees himself and shows the way to others.
~Mahatma Gandhi

Chapter 1

Various colors stained the wall of the tiny room where Kwil practiced his magic. As they slid down the wall and puddled on the floor, the various magics came together, popping and fizzing as they met. Kwil approached with caution, choosing his steps with care. *Master will be furious if he sees this,* he thought.

Kneeling down near the mess, he waved a hand lightly above it. A force field appeared above the mixing colors, neutralizing the magic inside. Fading into nothingness, the magic disappeared before his eyes. *At least that spell works the way it should.* With a sigh, the young man stood back on his feet and returned to his duties.

Kwil had long believed himself destined for great things. His heart yearned to study magic, and despite the fact that entrance to the Wizard's College was forbidden to him, he still considered himself a wizard. After all, he had studied every book he could get his hands on, and he practiced at every opportunity. Why should he be denied his education? He had already proved himself worthy to enter the College. From a very young age he displayed a talent for magic. He should have been given his place and allowed to learn.

Unfortunately, Kwil was born a slave. He was a mere human destined to serve a superior race. The Gatans considered themselves above all other species inhabiting Nōl'Deron, and as a result, they enslaved all others who came to their land. No species was safe, and none ever returned. As far as the outside world was concerned, the land of Gi'gata did not exist. There were only stories of a land of fantasy and mystery, where few dared to travel.

Kwil's parents had traveled aboard a ship that set out to find the mythical land. Though no ship ever returned after making such a voyage, the wandering spirit got the better of many people. Unsure which land his parents had originated from, Kwil could only guess at his true origins. Wherever they sailed from, his parents had met a fate that awaited many ships that sailed too near the waters of Gi'gata. They were attacked, taken prisoner, and forced to serve as slaves to the Gatans.

Vaguely remembering his mother's face, or at least the woman he believed to be his mother, Kwil would often compare himself to her. His own eyes were blue, his hair dark, and his skin rather pale considering his long stints of service out of doors. With ears that stuck out slightly from the side of his head, he knew he wouldn't be considered handsome, even for a human. The face he remembered, however, was lovely. She had golden hair and deep brown eyes, and she sang to him in a soft voice. The image of her face brought with it a sense of peace and warmth, and he took comfort in it whenever he felt low.

His father was unknown to him, but he was certain he must favor him in looks. How else could such a beautiful woman give birth to a child such as him? His father had been a lucky man indeed. Kwil didn't need to worry about attracting the opposite sex. It was unlikely he would be of interest to slave breeders. Looking down at the plain white shirt and woolen breeches he wore, he felt inadequate, even for a slave. He was slight of build, and as far as anyone else knew, untalented. Love was not allowed among slaves, so Kwil didn't give much thought to the slave girls he encountered. It was likely for the best. Passing on his magical tendencies to offspring could be dangerous.

With the colors of his magic swept away, he turned his attention to the duties he was supposed to be performing. Stepping outside the door of his quarters, he dropped his pretense as a wizard and assumed his true role as a slave. First, as always, he had to collect water for the family he served. They would insist on cleaning themselves before breakfast, and the punishment would be severe if their baths were not ready.

Moving through the darkened corridor, Kwil found his way outside. The well was not far from this side of the manor, and he was glad of it. A chill had settled in the air through the night, and he would not be given thicker winter garments for another month or so. Taking great care not to splash any water on himself, Kwil filled two buckets and carried them inside.

Fetching water was among Kwil's earliest memories. He had always been slender, and it was believed that by forcing him to carry water, he would become muscular and strong. Unfortunately his body had other ideas. He fell often, spilling the water and earning himself a beating. No matter how hard he tried to be large and strong, he was physically incapable. As he had grown over the years, he hoped to at least be tall. That too eluded him. His height was average for a slave, slightly shorter than most Gatans.

Carefully opening the door, Kwil smiled to himself. He hadn't spilled a single drop. He might not be the strongest, but he was meticulous and efficient— qualities required of a proficient wizard. Filling his masters' baths would require at least a dozen more trips, and that would give him time to concentrate on memorizing his spells. Though having a moment to read was rare, he would soak up any magic words he found and repeat them in his head as he went about his chores. That way he would not forget, and perhaps another day he would learn what the words meant.

Magic came as naturally to Kwil as any reflex. Though he had been warned by other slaves to hide it, he desired more than anything to let the magic flow. Humans in Gi'gata were forbidden to perform magic. Death was the immediate sentence for any slave suspected of doing so. It was widely rumored that humans weren't intelligent enough to practice magic, but the Gatan leaders were no fools. They were well aware that humans of other lands practiced magic freely, and that their own slaves were quite capable of learning. To avoid a rebellion, they kept their slaves ignorant, refusing to allow them to learn to read or have any education worth speaking of.

Kwil had been lucky in that regard. His failure to develop muscles had led to the easier job of brushing horses for an elderly Gatan woman. She was quite eccentric and insisted that her slaves make no noise in her home. One day while in the gardens, her eye fell on Kwil. She noticed the easy gait with which he moved, and his gentle nature with her horses. She favored him and invited him into her home. For years he served this woman, always taking careful steps and tiptoeing as he went to avoid disturbing her. When she fell ill, she insisted he tend her at her bedside. She helped him learn to read, and eventually insisted he read all of her correspondence aloud to her as she lay abed. With her constant corrections, he learned to read difficult words, and to speak clearly and eloquently. As her mind deteriorated, she mistook him for her own son.

Kwil's memories of his mistress were mostly good. Though she had been demanding at first, she rarely punished him or any of her other slaves. Her tenderness toward him at the end of her life had been alien to him. No one had ever spoken to him so kindly, nor cared whether he learned to read. Her last words to him had been a whispered "I love you, my son," which had stuck with Kwil ever since. Though it's doubtful she would have uttered those words had she been in her right mind, it was nonetheless special to him.

After his mistress died, her estate was divided among her real descendants, who brought in their own slaves. Kwil's services were no longer needed, and he was sold to Lord Orva. Rumors of Lord Orva's cruel treatment of his slaves had not escaped Kwil's ears. It was said that a graveyard existed near the manor, full of the slaves Orva had personally murdered. Kwil was unperturbed.

He was a hard worker, and he would adapt to Orva's expectations in order to survive. Holding to the dream that one day he would become a great wizard, Kwil's outlook on life was not as grim as other slaves. A bright future awaited him, he was certain of it.

As he reached the steps, he took great care to balance the water buckets on each side of him. One splash of water on the stairs would render them slick, and if his master should fall, Kwil shuddered to think what might be in store for him. Carefully placing each foot, he climbed to the fourth floor, where his master and mistress resided. Their rooms, which occupied the entire floor, consisted of separate bedchambers, two sitting areas, a trophy room—where Lord Orva's prized dead animals hung upon the walls—and two separate bath chambers.

Kwil made his way along the corridor, his eyes ever looking down. Making eye contact with his master without permission would lead to trouble. He learned upon their first meeting to follow the lord's rules. Kwil had been brought before his master along with three other slaves he had worked with previously. Lord Orva barely looked at them before ordering them to be whipped. "A reminder never to cross me," he had called it. Kwil had been dragged outside, his arms bound to a post, his shirt ripped from his back. Three lashes were more than enough, the spiked leather straps tearing into his flesh. The pain was excruciating, and the bruising lasted for weeks. Kwil would not forget it. Though he refused to live in fear, he made note of his master's ill temper. He would mind his duties carefully to avoid Lord Orva's wrath.

The following three months had not been all bad. Kwil steered clear of both master and mistress, doing only as he was told and making himself scarce. Rarely did he encounter either of them, and he intended to keep it that way. As long as he remained unnoticed, they would likely leave him in peace.

Emptying the bucket into Lady Orva's tub, he was startled by a maidservant who trotted past him. She was Gatan, a paid servant rather than a slave. Her sleek feline form moved silently across the room, adding rose petals to the tub before scurrying away. She barely noticed Kwil's presence, as if the tub were filling itself. He quickly dumped the second bucket before heading back downstairs to repeat the procedure.

As he reached the top of the steps a voice called to him. "Don't forget to heat the last few," the maidservant reminded him.

He turned to face her, bowing his head that he understood. This was the same reminder she gave him each day. How could he possibly forget? A cold bath would probably earn him more lashes, and he hoped to avoid any and all forms of punishment. Perhaps the young woman thought humans were too stupid to remember a daily task, or maybe she felt duty-bound to speak to him. Whichever it was, the pity in her yellow eyes was unmistakable.

Silently he walked back outside, lowering his buckets into the well and filling them. This time, he took the buckets to the fire pit, which the stable hands had already lit. He hooked the buckets a few inches above the flame, allowing the water to heat. If only he knew the correct spell, this work would be much faster. So far, he could do little more than manipulate objects at a distance. Looking around to be sure no one was watching, he gently waved a hand, summoning the smoke toward him. Twisting and shaping, he moved the smoke into spiral patterns, eventually swirling it into the shape of a rose. A half-smile came over his face, but the sound of approaching footsteps forced him to abandon his work. Waving the smoke away, he spun around, grabbing two more buckets.

When both baths were finally full and warm, he made his way downstairs to the kitchen area. He hadn't eaten since midday yesterday, and his rumbling stomach reminded him that he could not live on dreams of magic alone. Jenn, the elderly slave woman who ran the kitchens, smiled warmly at the young man's approach. Taking two biscuits from the tray in front of her, she shoved them in his hand and mussed his hair.

"Dear boy," she said as she turned back to her work.

Kwil took a bite of one biscuit and observed a moment as Jenn went about her work. She hummed as she dawdled through the kitchen, checking various dishes as they simmered or baked. She took pride in her kitchen, despite being forced to work in it. Here was a true example of making the best of one's situation. Kwil felt a fondness for the old lady, and she reminded him of his former mistress in many ways. She was kind to him, and even among fellow slaves, that was not easy to find. Many of them felt their work was a competition, fearing that a younger man might outshine them.

Kwil had encountered opposition so far only from those who worked outdoors, likely because they felt he had a more comfortable position working inside the manor. They were probably right, but Kwil could not trade places if he wanted to. The master told the slave where he would work, and the slave obeyed without question.

Before Kwil could vacate the kitchen, Lady Orva happened to appear in the dining room. Her black and brown fur was slightly disheveled, her green eyes showing signs of fatigue. It would seem she planned to eat before enjoying her bath this morning. Kwil knew what that meant—he had better keep the water hot.

As he turned to leave, Jenn nudged him gently. "She's with child," she said.

"Are you sure?" Kwil asked, wondering how much extra work an infant meant for him.

"If I had a coin, I'd wager it," the old lady said with a crooked smile.

Kwil nodded. She would certainly know better than him.

As if reading his mind, Jenn looked up from her cooking pot and said, "Don't worry. They'll hire on new staff for the kit." Reaching into her pocket, she said, "I almost forgot." She handed him a small bundle.

With a nod of gratitude, he peered inside the bundle to see fresh grapes. His eyes went wide. Normally his meals consisted of day-old bread and a handful of raisins if he was lucky. "Thank you!" he said, wrapping an arm around the old woman's neck.

"Off you go," she said, waving a hand to shoo him away.

Stuffing the bundle into his shirt pocket, he scurried back outside. *Today will be a good day*, he told himself.

A horn blasted behind him, breaking him from his reverie. Spinning around, he spotted Lord Orva, perched atop his destrier. He was a large man, who preferred a large, impressive horse when he rode out on the hunt. The tigerlike stripes of his face gave him the look of a fierce hunter. Kwil stepped aside as the lord and his friends galloped past without so much as a glance his direction. Listening to the thunder of footfalls as they moved farther and farther away, Kwil knew how he'd be spending the afternoon—cleaning and processing whatever his master managed to catch. Magic would have to wait for another day.

Chapter 2

"Boy!" Lady Orva called.

Kwil nearly dropped the bundle of laundry he was carrying. Lady Orva rarely came downstairs except to eat, and she had spoken no words directly to him since his arrival at the manor. He dipped his head, a sign that he was listening for her command.

"My daughter is returning home from school this evening," she said. "Make sure her room is spotless!" With those words, she twirled her skirts and headed back up the stairs.

Kwil was not aware the couple had any children, other than the one on the way. He'd never been asked to clean the rooms on the third floor, likely where the girl's room was located. The second floor was reserved for guests, and Kwil was very familiar with those.

Bundling the washing under one arm, Kwil pushed open the front door and stepped outside. The weather was pleasant, with few clouds present in the sky. It would be a good day to help with the horses, but it was unlikely any daylight would remain when he had finished cleaning. Making his way past the gardens, he headed toward the large tubs where the laundresses were busy scrubbing garments and hanging them on the line to dry.

"What's this?" a heavy servant asked. She placed her hands on her hips and stared at the young man. She was a Gatan and had little patience for human slaves. Kwil had encountered her almost daily, and she never bothered to speak a kind word to him.

"Laundry," he replied, extending the bundle toward her.

"You been wearing these fine dresses?" she asked, cackling with laughter.

Kwil did not reply. He remained silent, still holding out the bundle for the woman to take. After a few moments of looking him over, she said, "Don't give it to me. Take it over there." She gestured with a plump thumb toward another servant.

Without a word, Kwil moved forward and approached the girl. She was a young Gatan who barely looked at him as he approached. Reaching out her thin hands, she relieved Kwil of his burden.

"You can bring them straight to me from now on," she said in a quiet voice. "There's no need to bother Sal."

Kwil nodded his understanding, unsure if the Gatan wished him to reply verbally. A glance at her eyes suggested she was kind but shy. She avoided his gaze but showed no anger that he had looked at her. Before he could get himself into trouble, he marched on, avoiding the heavy laundress as he went.

Keeping his head down for fear of running into someone, Kwil moved up the manor steps. Another servant passed him, but she paid him no heed. Stopping on the third floor, Kwil raised his head and looked at the area before him. Rows of paintings hung on the walls, all of them depicting families with young children. As he moved along, he observed their faces, deciding that they must be relatives of the Orvas. Their fur came in a wide variety of colors, as was common among Gatans. Sometimes the children looked like their parents, and sometimes they looked entirely different.

One painting featured an unruly child, which the artist had chosen to depict truthfully. He appeared to be tugging at his mother's tail, the expression on her face showing her chagrin. Kwil couldn't suppress his amusement, and he laughed out loud, the sound echoing from the walls. Quickly slapping a hand over his mouth, he turned his head to see if anyone had heard. To his relief, no one was there.

There were only two doors on the third floor, and he hurried toward the one on the left. To his delight, it appeared he had chosen correctly. Inside was an abundance of furniture, all covered with white sheets to keep away the dust. Shaking out the sheet that covered the bed, he observed the plushness of the mattress beneath. Placing his hand on the bed, he pushed down, wondering what it must be like to sleep in such luxury.

As he looked around, he observed a thick layer of dust on every sheet. This was exactly the sort of task he was waiting for. Returning to the door, he focused his mind to the latch, willing it to move into position. With an audible click, the door locked. Kwil smiled to himself, satisfied that no one would enter and find him practicing magic. Cracking his knuckles, he positioned his hands and looked at the sheet covering the desk. Slowly the sheet began to move, drawing itself away from the furniture beneath. It hung briefly in midair before dropping to the ground.

Kwil frowned, wondering what had gone wrong. This was a spell he performed often, and he shouldn't have had any trouble with it. Bending to pick up the fallen sheet, he sneezed, blowing dust all around him. Could a layer of dust be inhibiting the sheet's movement? It seemed far-fetched, but he knew little of the intricacies of magic. It was possible that many minute details could affect it.

Deciding to clear the dust away first, Kwil reached for a broom. As he gripped the handle, he realized that dust was no different from any other object. In fact, it was much smaller and lighter. Focusing his mind, he concentrated on the dust that had settled upon the sheet covering a nearby chair. The dust rose in a small cloud, the gray particles dancing and swirling as they moved. Kwil fought back his excitement as it floated across the room, making its way to a trash bin in the corner. As it fell in place, Kwil celebrated quietly to himself. Next, he lifted the formerly dusty sheet, bringing it carefully to his arms to be folded. The delicate work of folding the sheet could not be done with magic. At least, not yet. Fine movements were difficult, and it took a lot of practice. If he had days to clean the room, he would certainly give folding a try. For now, he was content with moving dust and sheets.

Kwil continued cleaning in this manner, celebrating small victories, and confounding himself with his failures. With no master wizard to guide him, he might never perfect his art, but that didn't stop him from trying. The cleaning went on for hours until a rattling came from the door. His concentration broken, the final bits of dust scattered across the bedroom floor.

"Who's in there?" a female voice asked from outside the door.

Rushing to the door, Kwil quickly opened the latch and lowered his head.

"About time," the woman said. She leaned down to look at his face. "You new here?" she asked.

Kwil nodded, taking his first look at the lady before him. She was a youthful Gatan with tricolored fur. Flecks of gold highlighted her darker sections, and splashes of white added personality to her coat. Instead of the dresses worn by most women, she wore a buff-colored blouse with brown trousers. Her pale green eyes stared at the young man intently.

"Do you always lock the door when you're cleaning?" she asked, observing the stack of neatly folded sheets.

"Forgive me, Mistress," he said.

"Pffft," she replied, waving her hand. She shoved her way past him, gently setting a wooden case on her bed. As she placed a bundle of books on her desk, she said, "Call me Nera, not Mistress."

Kwil stammered over his words, unsure of the correct way to reply. "It is forbidden," he managed to say.

"Then call me that when no one else can hear you, okay?" she replied. "Looks like you missed a spot," she added, grinning and pointing to the dust pile on the floor.

Kwil quickly dropped to his knees and swept up the dust, placing it inside the bin. Bundling the sheets, he bowed and made his way back to the door. Shifting the load to one side, he reached for the door. As his arm lifted, he bumped into the books piled on the desk, knocking two of them to the floor. Immediately he dropped to retrieve them, his eyes falling on the titles of the books. All of them were about wizardry.

Gently caressing the covers as he placed them neatly in a stack, he could hardly pull himself away. Here before him was the information he desperately craved, information that could teach him how to properly cast spells.

"Have you finished yet?" Nera called from behind him.

Seduced by the sight of the books, he had momentarily forgotten where he was. Clearing his throat he replied, "Yes, Mist—Nera."

Nera smiled. "Close the door on your way out," she commanded. Turning her back to him, she focused her attention to the case on her bed.

Kwil took one more longing glance at the books before exiting. Pulling the door shut behind him, his hand rested a moment on the handle. He must find a way to read those books, even if it meant stealing them. Being caught could cost him his life, but without those books, he would feel as if he'd died anyway. The magic inside those pages called to him, beckoning him to the knowledge within.

* * * *

For several hours, Kwil busied himself scrubbing every inch of Nera's washing room. Unable to concentrate long enough to use magic, he worked directly with his hands instead. Only steps across the corridor was the knowledge he craved. How could he steal the books without causing suspicion? And where could he possibly hide them? Shaking his head, he tried to force the idea away. With Nera back home, it was likely he'd be sent daily to tend her room. That would be his chance to read while leaving the books where they belonged.

Back and forth Kwil moved his mop over the same spot of floor he had already cleaned. Nera had to leave her room eventually. Even if there was no time to learn this evening, he wanted to touch the books at least one more time before going to bed. Hoping she would demand a change of bedclothes or that something hadn't been completed to her liking, he waited for her voice to call out to him. To his disappointment, she did not.

After what felt like an eternity, he heard a small click of a door. Peeking out into the hallway, he saw Nera walking away. *It must be dinnertime*, he realized. His stomach was tied in knots, so he hadn't become hungry yet himself. The only nourishment he craved was in those books. Leaning out to observe, he watched as Nera made her way to the stairs and disappeared out of sight. This was his chance.

Dropping his mop to the ground, he raced across the hallway and let himself into the young woman's room. The books lay unmoved on the desk where he had left them. Snatching up the first volume, his eyes greedily ran over the pages as his heart pounded against his chest. This particular book focused on basic elements, magic that was unknown to Kwil. As he skimmed the pages, he caught snippets of advice on pulling magic from the elements that surround a wizard. Such magic seemed practical, but Kwil felt no connection to any element. How did one discover which element controlled his powers? Continuing to flip through the pages, he saw passages about wizards who could manipulate two or more elements. Smiling to himself, he hoped he would be able to do that someday.

Moving on to the next book, his eyes drank in the title: *A Beginner's Guide to the Arcane*. Clutching the volume to his chest, he knew he had found gold. Carefully opening to the first chapter, he stared at the words on the page. The writing was in the common tongue, but the spells were written in foreign characters, followed by a pronunciation guide. To his great disappointment, he realized he needed to go further back and study the correct language. The other two books on the desk were written in this language as well. Where would he find something that could teach him these words?

With a sigh, Kwil nearly set the beginner's book aside, but his hand would not let go. Taking a deep breath, he opened it once more and flipped to the first lesson. It was simple enough, naming a single word that would allow the reader to flip pages without touching the book. Stumbling in his attempt to pronounce the incantation, Kwil expected nothing to happen. His eyes went wide as the page flipped. Grinning ear to ear, he repeated the word to flip another page.

Considering himself lucky that the pronunciation guide was so well written, he moved on to the next spell. Along with an incantation, it presented a guide for the movement of the wizard's hand. It explained how to move one's fingers at the appropriate parts of the incantation. This would allow him to turn to any page he desired in his books. *Leave it to a wizard's school to teach you to study magic by using magic,* he thought. If a student incorporated magic into every aspect of his life, he would surely grow accustomed to it. Eventually, he could perform these spells without thinking. Kwil could only imagine what it would be like when he reached that point. These books could lead him there.

Slowly he spoke the words, attempting to move his fingers along with the rhythm of the spell. Nothing happened. Frowning, he tried again, but this time was no different. As he began the third try, the door swung open behind him. Dropping the book, he spun around to see Nera holding a small plate of food.

Hurrying to his feet, he tucked the volume away neatly on her desk and bowed his head. How much had she heard? What would she do to him? Silently he hoped she would not tell her father. Kwil would rather be turned over to authorities than face Lord Orva. He was a cruel man, and there was no telling what punishment he would have in store for a slave attempting to learn magic.

"I didn't realize slaves were allowed to read," she said, setting her plate on the desk.

"I wasn't reading, Nera," Kwil lied. "I was only straightening the books."

Nera narrowed her eyes as she observed the slave. "I heard you pronouncing the words," she said. "You were reading." Looking around the room, she added, "Everything in here is perfectly straight, just as you left it earlier. There was no need for you to return." In a more accusing tone, she said, "I saw the pages move when you cast the spell."

Kwil felt the redness creep into his face. "Please, Mistress," he said. "I meant no harm." Breathing heavily, he kept his head downward, staring at his feet.

"Relax," she said, picking up the book. "You want to learn magic?"

Kwil's head shot up, staring at the Gatan. "More than anything," he said, his voice a hoarse whisper.

The corners of Nera's mouth turned up, her face showing no sign of suspicion. "I don't want to learn it," she said. "My parents are forcing me to attend the College." Trotting over to her bed she opened the wooden case and pulled out a lute. Leaning back against her pillow, she strummed at the strings. "I prefer music, but that isn't smart enough for my parents."

"You're a free woman," Kwil replied. "Why not just do what you love?" The idea that a Gatan couldn't choose her own path was alien to him. A slave had no choice, but a highborn lady certainly had one.

"Papa would likely send me away if I left school," Nera responded. "What he doesn't realize is, there are other ways to make magic besides casting spells. And music is much more fun than memorizing spells all day."

Kwil didn't have an answer. Instead he stood silently for several minutes as Nera played a soft tune. He gave a quiet applause as she finished. "Can you sing?" he asked.

"Not very well," she replied honestly. "You?"

"Afraid not, Mistress," he said.

"Stop calling me that. I already told you my name is Nera."

"Of course, Nera," he corrected. "Forgive me."

Setting her lute aside, she sat up on her bed and looked at him. "You can't take the book from here," she said. "If anyone catches you with it, well I don't have to tell you what will happen."

Kwil nodded. Once again he would be cut off from learning, thanks to his lowly status.

"What you can do," she began, "is study it here with me."

His jaw dropping open, Kwil could barely take in a breath. Was she serious? She was going to help him learn?

"I'm not very good at it," she continued, "so I won't be much of a teacher. But you can study while I play my lute. That way no one will hear your voice when you pronounce the incantations."

His eyes filling with tears, Kwil fought the urge to grab the girl and hug her. Such an act would be completely inappropriate, but he felt an almost overwhelming sense of gratitude toward her. "Thank you, Nera," he said. "Thank you and thank you." Not knowing what else to say, his words trailed off.

"You're welcome," she replied. "You can begin now if you like."

Kwil jumped at the opportunity, eagerly grabbing the book and situating himself in a corner out of her way. Today was the beginning of his true life. Finally he had the chance to learn and develop the magic that lingered inside him, yearning to be set free.

Chapter 3

Each day Kwil spent more time in Nera's room, reading and practicing the magic written in the pages of her books. He learned a variety of simple spells, and he felt a sense of pride he had never experienced before. After only a week, he was finished with the beginner's book and ready to move on to the others.

"You're going to catch up to me," Nera commented playfully. Most days she took little interest in his studying. She simply sat upon her bed, strumming her lute while he read and practiced. Today, she seemed eager for him to demonstrate what he'd learned.

"I doubt that," Kwil replied, looking at the books. "I have a long way to go."

"But you catch on quickly," she said. "If you could read the runic symbols, I bet you'd learn twice as fast."

"Can you teach me?" Kwil asked eagerly.

Nera shook her head. "I don't know it, but I'm supposed to learn this year at the College."

Kwil's heart nearly stopped. She was only on break from her studies, and she would have to return in another week. She'd take her books with her, and he would be left with no way to continue learning.

Not noticing the slave's worried expression, Nera said, "Maybe you could come to school with me."

Stunned, Kwil stared up at her, wondering how such a thing was possible.

"Not as a student," she explained. "Second year students are allowed private chambers, and many of them bring a slave to serve them while they study. It frees up time to concentrate on studying—or playing the lute." The last bit she added with a grin.

"I would love that," Kwil replied.

"I'll have to ask my parents," she said. "But I think I can convince them to let me take you."

As she spoke, her eyes glanced over at the fireplace, where the fire had dimmed and was nearly out. She started to get up, but Kwil beat her to it. He leapt to his feet, hurrying to tend the dying embers.

"Forgive me," he said. Neglecting his duties was unacceptable, especially when it came to Nera. He owed her everything, and he felt pangs of guilt at allowing her room to grow cold.

Nera looked thoughtfully at the slave. "You know, the attitude toward slavery is changing in Gi'gata."

A bright fire roared to life before Kwil turned to face her. He wrinkled his brow, puzzled as to what she was talking about.

"News rarely reaches these sleepy country manors," she continued. "But in the city, many Gatans are no longer comfortable owning other living beings. It's an archaic and barbaric practice."

Kwil couldn't believe what he was hearing. "If we don't work for them, what do we do?" he wondered.

"Well, I've heard that many are sent back to their original homelands," she replied.

"Many slaves are born here," he stated. "I was."

Nera paused a moment, not sure how to reply. Sure he had an ancestral home, but he had never been there. Would it be right to free a slave and send him back to a land he'd scarcely even heard of? What would happen if freed slaves chose to stay? How would her people treat them? "Maybe those who don't wish to leave could be given jobs," she said.

"I already have a job," Kwil replied. The thought of being turned loose scared him. He had nothing—no money, no home, and no family. Should all slaves suddenly be set free, he would be doomed. Freedom didn't mean equality. Studying at the College would still be out of the question.

With a sigh, Nera said, "Look, I don't have all the answers. I only mentioned it because I thought you might like to know. Your future might be something better than serving my family." She managed a sweet smile, hoping she hadn't made him too uncomfortable. "Come on," she said. "I'll help you with your studies."

With a nod, Kwil returned to the books and flipped to the next lesson. Nera set her lute aside and watched with interest as Kwil manipulated the fire in the hearth.

"You didn't need to get up to tend that," she said with a laugh.

Kwil shrugged, his face slightly bewildered. "I didn't realize I could do that," he replied.

"How did you develop an interest in magic anyway?" Nera wondered.

"Since I was very small, I've been able to move things," he said. "And I can create colors in the air," he added, wishing he hadn't mentioned it. It was an unpractical and frivolous use of magic, but he enjoyed it.

"Show me," she said.

Focusing on the air in front of him, he waved his fingers in a delicate pattern. A shimmering butterfly of pink, yellow, and blue appeared before him. It flapped its wings, floating softly to sit upon Nera's knee. She looked up at the young man, her eyes bright.

"It's beautiful," she said.

As Kwil looked at the ground, the butterfly dissolved into a puddle of colors. "It's silly," he replied, shaking his head. "But it was the first bit of magic I managed to control," he explained. "And it's fun."

"That's because you created it," she replied. "You didn't just move it around, you conjured it from nothing." Picking up her lute, she added, "That's just how it is when you create music." She plucked at the strings and hummed a merry tune. Looking up, she said, "There's more to life than what you can learn in books."

Though her statement was true, Kwil saw no other way to learn the basics than through study. "Music requires study too, doesn't it?"

"Yes it does," she replied. "And lots of practice. No different from magic, really."

As she continued to play her music, Kwil turned back to the book and practiced a few more spells. The hand gestures were becoming more difficult, requiring more-delicate movements in time with the incantation. Growing frustrated, he wondered if he would ever get the hang of it.

Noticing his difficulty, Nera took a seat on the floor next to him. "Like this," she said, taking a hold of his hand. His skin was the roughest she had ever felt, and a glance at his fingertips revealed reddened blisters and cuts. "What happened?" she asked, not seeing the obvious answer.

Kwil looked at his fingers, unsure what she meant. "What happened to what?" he asked.

"Your fingers," she replied. "They're so sore. Doesn't that hurt?"

With a shrug, he said, "I'm used to it. It's no different from a farmer who works with his hands."

"Farmers can afford gloves," she said quietly. A wave of guilt came over her, knowing that she was a part of this young man's suffering. Despite her current friendship with Kwil, she had been content to order around servants and slaves all her life. Something had to change. "From now on, I'll clean my own room while you study," she declared.

"Nera, it's my job," Kwil replied. "I don't mind."

"I've made up my mind," she stated. "Now let's see if we can get this right."

As she assisted him in performing the gestures correctly, the clock on her mantle chimed.

"I'd better go," Kwil said. "I'm supposed to help in the kitchen tonight. You have guests coming."

Nera rolled her eyes. A fancy dinner with her parents was an inconvenience she could do without. But if she tried to stay in her room when guests were present, her father would likely drag her down the stairs. "I guess I'll see you there then," she said.

* * * * *

Taking inventory of the rows of decadent foods in front of him, Kwil counted no fewer than seven courses. The Orvas' dinner guests would no doubt be delighted by the variety and quality of foods. Jenn had generously allowed Kwil to sample a few, many of them being far too rich for his stomach. A small taste was all he required to know the foods certainly weren't for him. A lifetime of a bland diet had not prepared him for the sweetness of chocolate or the texture of goose liver.

Making sure that each dish was covered, Kwil lit candles under the ones that needed to stay warm, and fanned the ones that needed to stay cool. It was not the most stimulating job in the kitchen, but it was better than scrubbing floors. Besides, he looked forward to seeing the night's entertainment. This would be the first dinner party he had witnessed since coming to work for the Orvas, and he wasn't sure what to expect. All he knew was, the more lavish the dinner party, the more respected the host.

Jenn floated by him, a twinkle in her aging eyes. Though she had lived her entire life a slave, her spirits were undaunted. Dinner parties were her specialty—a chance to show what she was capable of. Kwil couldn't help but smile as he watched the old lady darting to and fro with surprising grace and agility.

Behind him the young laundress approached, clearing her throat loudly to get his attention. Kwil startled at the sound, turning around quickly to see who was there. It was the same young Gatan he had met before, and he felt ashamed that he had not asked her name.

Thrusting a bundle of clothing toward him, she said, "These are for you."

Taking the green and yellow tunic from her, his brow furrowed in confusion. "For me?"

The Gatan crossed her arms and sighed in frustration. "You don't think they'd want you in front of their guests dressed like that do you?" Shaking her head, she walked away, leaving Kwil behind to ponder her meaning.

He looked down at the shabby clothing he wore every day, the elbows of his shirt nearly threadbare. Though he washed the garments as often as he could, he supposed they could be cleaner.

Jenn crept up behind him and patted him on the back. "In there, Son," she said, pointing to the cupboard.

With a nod of thanks, Kwil stepped inside and quickly changed into the fancy clothing he had received. The pants were slightly loose, obviously designed for a larger man, and the velveteen tunic with its gold trim felt scratchy against his skin. Plain cotton suited him far better, but he had no room to argue. These clothes meant he would be serving in the dining hall, not waiting in the kitchens to fetch supplies. He had anticipated a night of straining to see the entertainment, catching glances whenever he could. Instead, he would be up front, viewing firsthand whatever the Orvas had planned. The thought sent his heart racing.

When he exited the pantry, Jenn was waiting for him. She reached up and patted his cheek before smoothing out his tunic. "That's better," she said, her eyes shining brightly. "You have fun out there, but don't let them know it." A soft laugh followed as she turned around to tend the confections, stacking them neatly on a silver tray.

Voices sounded from the hall, signaling the servants that the guests had arrived. A passing Gatan shoved a pitcher of wine at Kwil, which he took gladly. Filling wine goblets was a simple enough task, and it would allow him to move freely about the room and observe the night's events. After a wink from Jenn, Kwil headed into the dining area, where the guests where laughing and talking. Another servant carried empty goblets on a silver tray, and Kwil decided to follow him, filling the cups as he went. Each guest accepted his drink graciously, not paying much attention to who was doing the pouring. As long as their goblets remained full, they were pleased.

Nera made an entrance wearing a long satin gown. She looked out of sorts, tugging at the tight bodice and grimacing in her mother's direction. Kwil felt pity for his friend, seeing how much she detested the fancy garment. During their days of study together, he had never seen her wear anything other than pants. For a noble lady, she lacked severely in refinement and poise. She was truly her own person, and she wouldn't be dictated by the mores of the day.

Kwil hazarded a glance in her direction, noticing that she did not have a cup. Grabbing one off the dining table, he hastened to her side, filling the glass and offering it to her. At first glance, she seemed annoyed, but realizing it was Kwil standing before her, her face broke into a smile. Clearly he wasn't the only one surprised to see a friend all dressed up. She said nothing, but her eyes sparkled with silent laughter. Kwil blushed slightly before moving away to tend the other guests.

As the night went on, the guests became louder and seemed to find the humor in every little story that was told. Their glasses ran over, thanks to Kwil keeping a close eye to make sure no one was thirsty.

Finally, Lord Orva stood, banging his fork against his goblet. "Bring on the entertainment!" he declared, to the delight of his guests.

Applause broke out, many of the guests jumping to their feet. Being shorter than most of the Gatans, Kwil angled his neck to get a better view. A spectacular display of magic shot toward the ceiling. Colors and shapes flew around the room, including a multitude of butterflies. Nera shot a glance in Kwil's direction as the butterflies darted past her.

Following the display, a troupe of dancers entered the room. Their feline bodies were painted a multitude of colors, some Kwil had never seen before. The cost of such dyes must have been astronomical, but the Orvas would spare no expense to impress their friends. The men and women danced gracefully, tossing each other into the air and performing tricks on the fly. Kwil watched in amazement, nearly forgetting his duties as wine bearer. It was of little consequence, though, as the guests could hardly look away either. Such a display of acrobatics was captivating, and the crowd fell silent enough to hear the tiniest squeak of a mouse.

When the dancers finished, a second round of colorful magic lit up the dining hall. The crowd broke into applause and whistled their approval at the performers. Kwil stared in amazement, his mind full of wonder. Only the drumming of a hand against the table snapped him back to reality. One of the guests held out an empty goblet.

Rushing to the man's side, Kwil quickly filled the cup and backed away, his head down. Making his way around the table, he continued filling goblets until his pitcher was empty, then ran to retrieve another.

Nera waited for his return, and then addressed her mother. "Mother, I'd like to take a slave back to school with me when I go. Since I'm in my second year, I'll be far too busy to tend my own affairs."

Lady Orva seemed unsure. "Surely the school can provide for your needs," she said. The cost of tuition was extremely high. In her mind, the school should provide ample servants to wait upon the students.

Lord Orva was not deaf to the conversation. He watched the exchange with interest, his goblet held close to his lips.

Nera tried again. "Mother, all the highborn ladies bring slaves with them to tend their private chambers." Turning to face her father, she asked, "I *will* have private quarters, will I not?" At this point, she knew she had her father's attention. He refused to be outdone or thought of as less powerful than any other lord. Out of pure ego, he would grant his daughter's request.

"You certainly shall," he said, a smug expression on his face. "You shall take a slave with you, and you shall have the finest rooms the College has to offer."

Many of the guests around the table nodded their approval and lifted their glasses to the lord's generosity. Kwil had worked his way around the table, adding more wine to Nera's goblet.

"This one will do," she said, gesturing to Kwil.

Without argument, her father gave a single nod to approve his daughter's choice. Nera shot a knowing glance at Kwil, who sucked in a quick breath and held it. The young woman certainly had a knack for manipulating her father, and it had worked to Kwil's advantage. He would soon be off to the Wizard's College, learning things he could only imagine.

Chapter 4

Less than a week after the dinner party, Nera made preparations to leave for school. All of her clothing, except for the dresses, would need to be packed, as well as her lute, extra strings, and as many music books as she could get her hands on. The Wizard's College considered music a waste of energy, and she would have few opportunities to escape to the city to purchase such items. She dreaded her upcoming workload as a second-year student, especially considering she had no natural inclination toward magic. If the subject matter at least interested her that would be something. Unfortunately, she had little to look forward to.

Kwil's presence would make things more fun, she decided. Over the past couple of weeks, she had come to enjoy his presence. She no longer thought of him as a servant. He was a trusted friend, one she could reveal her innermost thoughts to. Instead of chiding her for not trying harder to please her parents, he encouraged her to play music and perfect her art. He would even pause his reading just to listen to her newest compositions. Nera had no friend at the College she considered closer. In fact, she thought of the other students as mere acquaintances who would likely turn on her in an instant if the opportunity arose.

A light knock at her door alerted her to Kwil's presence. "Come in," she called, turning to greet him. He carried no bags and wore the same shabby clothing he always did. "Haven't you packed?" she asked.

"I've nothing to pack, Nera," Kwil replied.

Frowning, she asked, "You at least have a change of clothes for the journey, don't you? And it's getting colder out. You're going to need a cloak."

Moving across the room to tend the fire, Kwil replied, "I've never owned a cloak, and my other shirt is far worse than this one." With a shrug, he added, "Your parents will likely give me a thicker one once winter truly arrives."

With a sigh, Nera said, "I guess they wouldn't want you to freeze solid while you're fetching their bath water." She patted a finger against her cheek as she thought about what to do. "I'll have the seamstress make you some new clothes. She's always so fast." Before Kwil could reply, she bolted to the door and hurried down the stairs to find the seamstress.

Since the pair were due to depart the next day, Kwil doubted the seamstress could possibly craft anything so quickly. He would be presented to the College as a slave, which meant no one would care how he was dressed. In fact, with the majority of the population ignoring him entirely, he could run around naked and no one would notice. It was best not to argue with Nera, however, so he grabbed one of her books and took a seat by the fire.

Only a few pages into his studies, Nera returned. In her arms she carried several garments. A wide smile graced her lips. "She was already working on new clothes for the serving staff," she announced. "Here, see what you think of these." She lifted up the shirt on top and held it up for size. "It might be a little big on you, but it'll do."

Kwil brushed his fingers across the soft fabric. "This isn't for a servant," he replied.

Pressing a finger to her lips, Nera said, "Shhhh. Some of these are, but a few of them aren't." She drew a heavy gray cloak from the bundle. "This will keep you warm."

Taking the cloak, Kwil marveled at its fine quality. A riding cloak suitable for Nera herself, it was worth more than the price of a slave. "This is too fine a garment for me, Nera."

"Nonsense," she replied, plopping on her bed and grabbing her lute.

"If I'm seen wearing this, someone might think I've stolen it," Kwil said. No one would believe a lord dressed his slaves so well.

"Then only wear it when I'm around," she replied. "No one would dare question me."

Tears filled the slave's eyes as he looked at his friend. By allowing him to learn, she had already done more for him than any other being ever had. Now she was giving him even more. He felt as if he were her equal, at least for the time when they were alone together. Realizing that she didn't consider him her slave meant the world to him.

"What's the matter?" she asked, seeing his tears. Leaping up from her bed, she stood before him and wiped a tear from his cheek.

Not knowing what to say, Kwil wrapped his arms around her and squeezed her as tight as he could. To his delight, she reciprocated and laughed softly in his ear.

"I'm glad you like the clothes," she said, pulling away from him.

"I'm glad to have a friend," he replied. "I've never had one before."

Placing her hands on her hips, she stated, "I've never had a *real* friend before either. I don't fit in well among the nobles."

Wiping his eyes, Kwil smiled and attempted to lighten the mood. "I guess I have something to pack now," he said.

"Yes, you do," she replied. "Stuff them in this bag, and we'll pretend it's mine."

After finishing preparations for the journey, the two fell into their old routine. Nera fiddled with her lute while Kwil read quietly in the corner. Instead of sitting on the floor, he perched himself on one of Nera's cushioned chairs. Though she'd invited him to sit comfortably many times, he always insisted on staying on the ground, until tonight. For the first time, he felt deserving of a proper chair.

It was well into the night before the two parted company, Kwil returning to his tiny room in the manor's lowest level. The chill of early winter permeated the area, prompting many of the servants to double up for warmth. Luckily, no one was waiting in Kwil's bed. Pulling his thin blanket up to his chin, he drifted off to sleep knowing this would be the last cold night he would spend here. With Nera's help, he would someday become a wizard and leave his life as a slave behind him.

By morning, a well-rested Kwil made his way to the courtyard, where Nera's bags had already been loaded onto her carriage. The inner compartment stood empty, awaiting its valuable passenger. The coachman simply pointed as Kwil approached, letting him know he would be riding on the outside with the luggage. Unfazed, Kwil climbed aboard.

Moments later, Nera appeared in the doorway, her mother dabbing at her eyes with a handkerchief. Lord Orva stepped outside, wrapping an arm around his wife and waving goodbye to his daughter. Without delay, Nera climbed inside the carriage and peered out the back window toward Kwil. With a wink, she closed the curtain and waved to her parents.

A few miles down the road, Nera ordered the driver to stop and invited Kwil to sit inside with her. The coachman started to protest, but a cutting glare from Nera forced him to hold his tongue. It was no business of a servant what the lady wanted with the slave. The journey resumed with the two friends riding in the warmth of the carriage.

"Sit next to me and share my blanket," Nera said.

Kwil had taken the seat across from her to allow her some space but was glad to move next to her. Placing the blanket over his legs, he said, "Thank you. It was a bit cold out there."

"The coachman has a heavy coat to keep him warm," Nera said. "It isn't right they expected you to sit out in the wind in those thin clothes."

Nera reached for the small satchel she had brought inside the carriage. Pulling out a book of music theory, she laid it across her lap and reached back into the bag. Inside, she had the magic book Kwil had been studying. Handing it to him, she said, "Did you finish all of the others?"

Kwil nodded. In only two weeks' time, he had completed all the lessons in the first three books, and was more than halfway through the fourth. Even without fully understanding the new language, he could memorize and pronounce the spells correctly.

"Amazing," Nera said. "It took me the better part of a year to get through two of those, and I barely passed." Sighing, she added, "This year will be much harder. I might need your help." She flashed a weak smile before turning her attention to her own book.

The four-hour carriage ride was uneventful, and soon they were looking at the stone buildings that made up the Wizard's College. Students moved here and there, rushing to find the appropriate books and supplies before classes began the following day. Some of those running around appeared to be servants, likely running errands for their masters to spare them the added stress.

"Should I retrieve your supplies for you?" Kwil asked.

"No," she replied. "We'll take our stuff to the dormitory first, and then we'll go together. I probably have about a dozen books to track down, and who knows what else they want me to have?"

The carriage rolled to a stop outside one of the manor houses. "Help us with the bags," Nera told the coachman. Grabbing her small satchel, she allowed Kwil to grab two of her bags to keep up the appearance that he was her slave. The trio stepped inside, the servants waiting back while Nera inquired of the staff about her room. Returning to their side, she said, "Third floor, second door on the left."

The mansion had the highest ceilings of any building Kwil had ever seen. Even for an establishment built by the wealthiest nobles, he found the furnishings to be over the top. All of the chairs were decorated with scrolling golden embellishments, and the walls were adorned with golden candelabrums. The price of the candles alone, which were burning despite the brightness of day, had to have cost a fortune.

Trotting up the stairs single file, the trio found the room that would be Nera and Kwil's home for the next several months. The coachman placed the bags near the door, expecting Kwil to handle the unpacking.

"Thank you," Nera said. "You may go." With a bow, the Gatan spun around and walked away.

Kwil was amazed at the extravagance of Nera's room. Not only did she have a private bath, she had her own private library, stocked with various texts on magical subjects. A small servant's room attached to hers was at least three times the size of the room Kwil had at the Orva manor. Stepping inside, he took notice immediately of the feather bed, writing desk, and wardrobe.

"All of this is for me?" he asked.

Nera replied, "Some wealthy students bring Gatan servants. They typically get better sleeping areas than humans."

Kwil couldn't remember seeing any of the Gatan servants' quarters at the Orva manor. Those rooms were not on his list for cleaning, so he had no need to go there. Setting his bag aside, he laid down on the mattress. "I've never slept anywhere so comfortable," he declared. In fact, he wasn't sure if he'd be able to sleep. His bones only had the experience of sleeping on a thin mat on top of a stone floor. Too much comfort might not agree with them, but he was happy to give it a try.

"Obviously there's no fireplace in there, so you can sleep in my room if you get cold this winter. There's plenty of cushions, so take your pick."

Nera wasn't kidding. In addition to plush carpeting underfoot, every chair had at least three pillows. Apparently students liked to be comfortable while they studied. Kwil hadn't expected such lavish dormitories. A wizard was expected to study hard and stay clear of distractions, but after seeing the living area, it was hard to believe they'd be willing to leave their rooms long enough to attend classes.

"I need to pick up my books from the library," Nera said, tossing her bags to the side.

"I can put those away for you," Kwil offered.

"We'll do it later. Don't you want to see the library?"

"More than anything," Kwil admitted.

"Then let's go," Nera replied, patting him on the back. "Even though there aren't any music books in there, I have to admit the library is impressive."

Together they crossed the campus, Kwil taking in the sights and sounds. There were small gardens everywhere, likely growing herbs and other ingredients necessary to craft potions. A large pond sat at the center of the grounds, where dozens of benches allowed students to sit and ponder in peace. Several white swans danced upon the water's surface, stretching their wings and turning their faces to the sky. They were the prettiest birds Kwil had ever seen.

As they approached the library, Kwil's breath was stolen away. He paused, hoping to make the moment last a while longer. Its construction appeared ancient but well kept. The knowledge inside beckoned him, and he felt too overwhelmed to move.

"Come on," Nera said, nudging him forward. She grabbed the door handle and held it open for Kwil to step inside, a crooked grin on her face.

Stepping inside, Kwil's eyes grew wide with wonder. The smell of old pages met his nostrils, and he closed his eyes momentarily to enjoy it. When he opened his eyes again, he couldn't begin to count the vast number of tomes lining the walls. Hundreds upon hundreds of shelves filled the center of the room, and four staircases led to even greater wonders on the floors above. Paintings of famous Gatan wizards adorned the walls, each of them staring down at the simple slave who had so boldly entered their presence. Kwil, nearly euphoric, became dizzy as he attempted to look everywhere at once.

Lending a hand to steady him, Nera said, "Take it slow, Kwil. There's a lot to see." She could imagine herself having a similar reaction should she enter a vast collection of music. This was his idea of paradise, and she enjoyed seeing his reaction.

For over an hour, Nera followed along as Kwil moved through the stacks, peering at an assortment of books. Few people were around, so no one noticed that the slave was leading his mistress. Nera enjoyed his enthusiasm, and she happily carried the books he wished to borrow while he kept his hands free to flip through more. Eventually, she said, "There's a limit of ten."

Kwil hadn't realized how many he'd collected. "I'm sorry," he said, taking the stack from her. Scolding himself for being so thoughtless, he made a mental note to pay more attention. After all, he was the one who should be carrying her books, not the other way around.

"I'll just go grab my school texts and then we'll be off," Nera said. "You can wait by the door."

Nodding, Kwil carried the heavy stack of tomes toward the door and waited for his friend. When she returned, she was carrying six books of her own. "Now we can finish getting settled in," she said.

As they stepped out of the library, Kwil felt he was truly home. Here at his fingertips was all the information he could possibly desire. Thanks to Nera, he would have ample time to read and learn. With his friend at his side, he was no longer a slave—he was a wizard in the making.

Chapter 5

Within days of arriving at the College, Kwil and Nera settled into a routine. Kwil would study during the day while Nera attended classes. This allowed him to catch up to her, and she considered him at least as knowledgeable as any other second-year student. Every evening when she returned to her chambers, she would share with him what she had learned that day. Together they would complete her homework, and she was certain her marks would improve thanks to his help.

Nera always took meals in her room, sharing whatever the school was serving with her friend. In his entire life, Kwil had never been offered so much to eat, and his body reacted favorably to the additional calories. Though still thin, his face shone with a radiance of good health since he no longer lacked vital nutrients.

The runic language proved no match for Kwil's sharp mind. He excelled at the subject, reading incantations with ease. Nera had great difficulty until Kwil suggested she put the symbols to music. Though they still gave her fits, she found it easier to remember what each rune stood for.

With Kwil's help in her studies, Nera found herself with more time to spend on her music. The previous year, she had spent many long hours laboring over her schoolwork, which took away from what she really wanted to do. Now she could sit and play her lute every night, and her skills were improving. She challenged herself with more-difficult refrains, perfecting her technique and fine-tuning her own ear. Though she originally dreaded returning for a second year, she was glad she had made the decision to stay. She was enjoying her time with Kwil.

One evening while she was strumming away, a thought occurred to her. "You know," she began, "if you're going to have four years of basic wizard's training, that's going to force me to stay as well."

"You don't want to stay?" Kwil asked.

"Not at all," she replied. "I've frequently thought about running away." Clutching at her lute, she said, "All I want to do is make music, but that isn't good enough for my parents. They want a master wizard in the family." Laughing, she added, "Maybe they should adopt you."

Kwil laughed, turning to look out the window toward the lake. "I'd love to stay here forever," he admitted. "But if you decide to leave, then I'll leave with you." Turning back to face her, he said, "As long as I have some of these books and your friendship, I'll be fine wherever I am."

It was the kindest thing he could have said to her. She fought back her tears, and said, "That's very selfless of you, Kwil. You're a true friend." In her mind, he cared more for her than her own parents did. They were uninterested in her dreams, and they were determined to force her into a life that did not suit her. Kwil had been far more supportive and more family to her than they had ever been. All they seemed to care about was their own reputation among the wealthy. Having a musician for a daughter would bring shame on them, as the position was considered lowly and undesirable by the upper class. Despite the fact that nobles paid musicians to perform at their dinner parties, the musicians themselves were looked down upon. They could be entertaining, but they were uncivilized, as were all performers.

Nera didn't care what they thought of her. Becoming a wizard was not her desire, and ultimately, she would fail. Mastering the arcane required immense skill and too much study. If a student wasn't fully committed, he wouldn't succeed. Nearly any Gatan could learn basic spells, but to truly excel took dedication that she lacked. Only music mattered.

"Do you think you'll be content without becoming a master wizard?" she asked.

Kwil didn't need to think about it. "Who says I can't become a master? I may never have a title from the College, but that won't make me any less a wizard."

Narrowing her eyes, Nera replied, "You're wise for someone so young." Kwil's life experience was far different from her own, and she decided that was what had given him his determination. Having the odds stacked against him, he would be forced to work harder to overcome them. She could see the determination in his eyes and knew nothing would stand in his way. Gi'gata would not be big enough for him. Somewhere was a land that would accept him as he was, and Nera hoped one day to see him succeed there. All he needed was a proper teacher—someone who knew far more than she.

"How would you feel about talking to one of my teachers?" she asked. "Maybe one of them could be convinced to tutor you privately."

Kwil's heart jumped to his throat. "I don't think that's a good idea, Nera. Humans are forbidden from practicing magic."

"I know, but you deserve a proper teacher," she argued. "Besides, not all Gatans agree with that. Mistress Tress would probably agree to it. She's open-minded, and she owns no slaves."

Shaking his head, Kwil replied, "I still don't think it's safe. I'd rather stay as we are. I'm already learning more than I ever dreamed." The thought of confiding in someone else didn't sit well with him. The law was clear—any human practicing magic was put to death. There was no way to know how Nera's teacher would react.

With a sigh, Nera dropped the subject. Kwil was frightened, and that was only natural. But Nera knew Mistress Tress could be trusted. She was honorable and forward thinking. If any of the masters at the College would be willing to teach Kwil, it was she. If she didn't want anything to do with it, Nera trusted she would keep silent about Kwil's learning.

The following morning, Nera got herself ready for class with no obvious change in her demeanor. She didn't want to alert Kwil, who might talk her out of what she was about to do. Unable to focus on her lessons, she instead tried to decide which words she would use when approaching Mistress Tress.

Nera scanned her surroundings as she approached her teacher's office. Few students were around, most of them with their noses buried in their books. It was unlikely anyone cared to overhear what she had to say, so she pressed on toward the door and knocked.

"Enter," a voice called from inside.

Nera turned the handle and peered inside. Mistress Tress smiled and tucked away the lesson plans she had been preparing. Though Nera was not her finest student, she was a special girl with an endearing personality.

"What can I do for you?" Tress asked. She motioned for Nera to have a seat.

Seating herself across from the master wizard, she paused a moment, still trying to find the words she wanted to use. "I have this friend," she began, haltingly. "He, well, err…"

Tress folded her hands and rested her elbows against the desk. "You've come here for a reason, Nera." She flashed her student a smile. "Out with it."

Taking in a deep breath, Nera tried to calm her nerves. What would Kwil say if he knew she was here? She already knew the answer. He would beg her not to speak of him. Mustering her courage, she decided it was too late to go back. This was Kwil's only chance to become a true sorcerer. "I have a friend who is unable to study here at the College," she explained. "He's a promising young wizard, but his status won't allow him entrance."

Tapping a finger against her lips, Tress sat back in her chair. "I think I understand," she said. "Your friend is not of noble birth, and he hasn't the funds to attend classes."

"Yes," Nera replied, quickly looking away from her teacher's eyes.

"We do have scholarship programs for potential students who demonstrate significant talent," Tress stated. "Normally they require the sponsorship of a professor." Leaning forward, she added, "Mind you, it's rather difficult to be chosen for one of those scholarships. It's also infrequent. In my twelve years teaching, I've seen only one student granted any award money."

"If my friend could prove to you that he's ready, would you sponsor him?" Nera asked, her eyes hopeful.

"Perhaps," Tress replied. "I'd have to meet with him first and determine his skill level."

"He knows as much as I do," Nera declared. "He's taught himself everything."

"That is impressive," Tress replied, raising an eyebrow. "But I'm not sure that will be enough. The requirements for scholarship are set high. Probably too high."

"Could you tutor him?" Nera asked, almost pleading. "He learns quickly, and he won't take much of your time."

Tress sighed. "I'm not sure I have the time, honestly." Seeing the desperate look on her student's face, she asked, "When could I meet him? I have to talk to this person before I can decide anything."

Nera thought for a moment. "I suppose I could arrange a meeting today if you have time." Nera's voice grew thinner as she spoke. At some point she would have to reveal to Tress that her friend was a human slave. She was going to find out when she met him, and it would be better to know beforehand if that would be a problem.

Noticing Nera's frustration, Tress asked, "Is there something else?"

Shifting uneasily in her seat, Nera tried to decide what to say next. Racing through her mind were many different scenarios, most of them bad. Would Tress be willing to listen once she knew the truth? Would she be angry? Was it possible she would be open to the idea? Nearly panicking, Nera wondered if she should just drop the subject and leave now before things got worse. Before she could stand up, her teacher spoke again.

"It's all right, Nera," she said. "You can trust me."

Her words seemed sincere, and Nera wanted desperately to believe her. Steadying her breathing as best she could, Nera said, "My friend is a human."

Tress's jaw dropped open slightly, but she remained calm and silent. Nera's eyes darted side to side, searching for what to do next. A few moments of silence passed between the two as Tress processed the information. "Your human friend is skilled at magic?" she finally asked. "He has taught himself to do this?"

Nera's heart pounded in her ears as she replied, "Yes, ma'am." She felt a tightness in her throat as she realized what her teacher was thinking. Luckily, she had not mentioned Kwil's name or that he was the human working for her. It would not spare him from suspicion, but she might be able to convince her that she was speaking of some other human.

Crossing her arms, the master sorceress let out an audible sigh. "This is a serious crime, Nera. How could you be a part of something like this?"

Things had gone from bad to worse. Nera had expected Tress to be more open-minded and unlikely to have this reaction. The law was wrong, and Nera wanted nothing more than to shout that fact at the woman she had trusted. But that would not help the situation. Nera had already made a grave error, and now Kwil's life could be in danger. Staying calm was her only option. Perhaps she could control the damage she had done.

"I didn't realize it was a crime," Nera replied, attempting to save face. If Tress had her dragged away as a criminal, there would be no one to protect Kwil. The authorities would assume it was him she had spoken of, and he would be executed without a trial. And it was all Nera's fault.

"Come now," Tress said, not believing her. "You're a grown woman who has studied in the finest schools. You must be aware of the law."

Choosing her words carefully, Nera replied, "I knew it would be taboo and that most Gatans would dislike it, but I did not know it was a crime." Her only chance to avoid arrest was to convince her teacher she was ignorant of the law. She did not look away for fear Tress would see through the lie.

After a pause, Tress said, "All right, Nera, but you must tell me who this human is. He mustn't be allowed to perform magic unchecked. He is a threat to everything we Gatans hold dear."

Thinking quickly, she replied, "He was a slave in my friend's household."

Tress stared into Nera's eyes and said, "You're a terrible liar. The truth now."

Nera swallowed hard. "He was in my household, but my parents sold him before I left for school. I do not know his name."

"You're trying my patience, Nera," Tress said, anger rising in her voice. "If he was your friend, then you would know his name. I think you're protecting him, and you're playing a dangerous game."

Nera remained silent. What else could she say? She would never admit it was Kwil, even if it meant being thrown in prison or worse. She would not have his death on her conscience. Wishing she could turn back the clock and never come into Tress's office, Nera closed her eyes and breathed deeply.

"Fine," the sorceress said. "Every member of your household will be searched, beginning with the slave you brought with you."

Nera's eyes shot open, her muscles tensing.

"It's him, isn't it?" Tress asked. "Your reaction reveals everything."

"Please," Nera begged. "He's done nothing wrong!"

"You will turn him over to the authorities," Tress demanded. "Fetch him and bring him here, and we can do this quietly. I'd hate for your father to find out about this."

Nera knew she had no choice but to agree. Nodding, she replied, "I will. He's on an errand for me at the moment, but as soon as he returns, I will bring him to you."

"See that it doesn't take too long," Tress warned.

Tears splashed against Nera's cheeks as she nodded her agreement. "I won't keep you waiting long," she promised. Rising slowly from her chair, she exited the room, closing the door behind her. Wiping her eyes, she broke into a run, sprinting toward her dormitory. It was time to tell Kwil what she had done.

Chapter 6

Racing across the campus as fast as her paws could carry her, Nera barely took notice of the students in her path. She pushed them aside without remorse as she hurried to warn her friend. If she couldn't get him to safety before Mistress Tress sent the guards, they would both face severe punishment—and Kwil might lose his life.

Charging up the steps to her dormitory, she shoved open the door and stepped inside. Kwil hopped from his seat, a look of surprise on his face. Struggling to catch her breath, Nera crossed the room and took the book from his hands, tossing it on the bed.

"We have to go now!" she warned, still out of breath.

"What's happened?" he asked.

"I made a terrible mistake," she replied, turning her back to him. Grabbing at the bags in her closet, she flung them out onto the floor and began shoving clothes inside one. "Bring whatever you need, but not too much."

"I don't think that'll be a problem," Kwil remarked, still uncertain what had occurred. He grabbed a bag and placed the clothes Nera had gifted him inside. Rolling up two blankets, he secured them to the bags before asking, "Can you tell me what happened?"

Nera paused momentarily. "I'm an idiot," she stated. "I told one of my teachers about you. I thought she was open-minded and would agree to help you learn." Shaking her head, she said, "She's just like all the others, and I put your life in danger by speaking to her." Rushing to Kwil, she took his hands in hers. "Can you ever forgive me? I've ruined everything." She hung her head, staring at the floor.

Kwil swallowed hard, realizing the idyllic life he had enjoyed here at the College was at an end. His secret was out, and now if he didn't leave, he would be put to death. Looking at Nera, he wondered what had prompted her to make such a decision. He had asked her not to speak of him to anyone, fearing that this exact scenario might occur. With a sigh, he said, "I understand why you did it, Nera. You wanted to help me." Reaching out, he hugged his friend close to his heart. How could he be mad at her? She had already risked so much for him, and she'd given him opportunities he never dreamed possible. He had already learned more over the past few weeks than in his entire lifetime.

Nera sobbed against his shoulder, grateful for her friend's forgiveness. "I'm so sorry," she repeated.

"There's no need to be," Kwil responded. "You've given me so much already."

Wiping away her tears, Nera said, "We'd better finish packing." She turned her attention to her lute, tucking it away neatly in its case.

"You could probably talk your way out of this," Kwil said. "I have to leave, but you could stay."

Nera looked up, wrinkling her brow. "Haven't you been listening all this time? I don't want to be a master wizard. I don't need this school."

"But your family," Kwil argued. "They'll be angry if you run away. You might never see them again."

Straightening her bag onto her back, Nera replied, "You're my family now, Kwil. My parents wanted an obedient child to bring them renown among their friends. That isn't me." Inside, she realized this meant she would never meet the kit her mother was carrying. The poor child would have to endure the same upbringing she had—one where she wasn't free to pursue her dreams. "My only regret will be not meeting my little brother or sister," she said. "But anything's possible, right?" Picturing the toddling little kit brought a smile to Nera's face.

Kwil nodded slowly, looking into his friend's eyes. How easily she would give up her comfortable life to join him in his exile. Each day she proved herself more and more his friend. "If you're sure," he said.

"Of course I am," she replied. With a smile, she added, "Do you think you could survive out in the wilderness without me?"

Kwil didn't know, and Nera had few skills for surviving in the wild either, thanks to her life as a noblewoman. Not once had she slept anywhere other than in luxury. Still, her determination was something to be admired, and Kwil knew he was better off with her at his side. "Let's get going then," he said.

"All right," she replied, "but you can't take all those books. Choose two that you haven't already read."

"I've read them all," he admitted.

"Then leave them," she said. "We'll find new ones. The destination I have in mind should be full of them."

Leaving the majority of her possessions behind, Nera led the way as the pair descended the steps and walked out onto the campus. "That's the shortest way to the road," she said, pointing to the east.

With a nod, Kwil continued to follow her lead. They passed the lake unnoticed, but when they decided to take a shortcut through some garden beds, the campus guards took notice. One of them shouted at Nera, prompting her to run.

"Run!" she shouted to Kwil. Tress could have already alerted the guards about her and Kwil, and she wasn't about to take any chances.

Kwil dashed along beside her, the guards giving chase for only a few yards before giving up. Trampling a garden bed wasn't too serious of an offense. Apparently Nera's teacher had kept her word to give her time to turn in Kwil herself. At least she wasn't a liar on top of being a bigot.

The pair made it safely to the road before stopping to look back.

"It isn't too late to change your mind," Kwil said.

Nera's shoulders dropped as she looked at her friend. "I told you I'm coming with you," she said. "If anyone saw a human running around loose, they'd assume you were a runaway slave. Who knows what they'd do to you?"

Seeing the logic in her argument, Kwil did not protest. He was happy for her company, but he felt bad that she would have to live a life of exile. Looking across the road, he peered into the woods. "Where do we go from here?" he asked. "I don't think those woods look too inviting."

"No, they don't," Nera replied. "We'll have to follow this road. It's only about twenty miles or so to the next town. Just past it lives a man who might be able to help us."

"Who?" Kwil wondered. "Can he be trusted?" After being forced to flee the College, he wasn't eager to trust any Gatan other than Nera.

Motioning for Kwil to follow, Nera began the long journey down the road. "He's something of an outcast," she explained. "Master Rili is his name, and he came from a poor upbringing. He had to prove himself to study magic." Pausing in her march, she placed a hand on Kwil's shoulder. "That makes him a kindred spirit."

"Our situations aren't exactly the same," he pointed out. "How do you know we can trust him?"

Continuing her march, she replied, "There are rumors he's part of a movement to end slavery in Gi'gata."

"But that's only a rumor," Kwil said, growing anxious. "How can you be sure?"

"I can't," Nera admitted. "But we have to try something. Our options are limited, and I think this is the best one." Her confident demeanor belied no trace of the doubt in her mind. How would Master Rili react to a slave seeking shelter? Nera couldn't say. All she knew was that Rili lived apart from others for a reason. He was a misfit, and those kind of people tended to stick together. Besides, if trouble reared its ugly head again, she was sure the two of them could outrun it. No city guards would patrol Rili's area, and it would take hours for him to fetch them. By then the pair would be gone, searching for a safe place to hide. Unfortunately, if Rili was not obliging, Nera had no idea where to turn next. That information she kept to herself.

As they moved along the dirt road, the clouds gathered overhead. A gentle mist soon gave way to a downpour, forcing the two to take cover beneath the trees.

"This is all we needed," Nera remarked.

"At least it will keep anyone from following us," Kwil said, looking on the bright side.

"I suppose so," she replied, pulling her cloak from her bag. Fastening the clasp around her neck, she pulled the hood over her head. "You should wear that cloak I gave you."

Kwil had forgotten he owned the garment. Rummaging in his bag, he pulled out the woolen cloak and wrapped it around his shoulders. The hood proved a fine barrier against the rain, which slowed after half an hour. The two took to their feet once more, their shoes sticking slightly in the mud as they walked.

A light drizzle continued to plague them, so they kept their hoods up for the next several miles. Only a few wagons crossed their paths, none of them stopping to inquire if the two would like a ride. Merchants were always wary of travelers who might steal their goods, and nobles in their carriages would offer no assistance to those who traveled by foot.

Trudging along on the muddy road, the two chatted to fill the silence. Nera spoke mostly of her music and the songs she intended to learn. Kwil listened intently, all the while trying to put the day's events behind him. He could not focus long enough to talk about magic. He was grateful to his companion for filling the gaps in their conversation.

Eventually the sun moved low in the sky and the rain relented, giving way to a cloudy, orange sky. With the ground too wet to camp for the night, the pair agreed to continue walking until morning, or until their aching feet forced them to stop.

As the sun disappeared from the horizon, Nera paused, throwing a hand in front of Kwil. Staring into the distance, she narrowed her pale green eyes.

"What is it?" Kwil asked. He did not share the Gatan's innate ability to see in low-light conditions.

"I saw figures moving among the trees," she said.

"Animals?" Kwil wondered. He had no idea what sort of wild creatures might dwell in the woods, and he wasn't sure he wanted to find out. If they were dangerous, he had no way of protecting himself or his friend. He had never held a weapon, and none of the spells he had studied were intended for fighting.

Nera shook her head. "They were Gatans," she replied. "They moved from the road to the trees. I don't see them now, but I don't think they went far."

Every hair on her neck stood up as she tried to steady her breathing. Whoever these people were, her gut told her they were not friendly.

Straining to see, Kwil couldn't make out anything except blobs that were probably trees. With the moon hidden behind the clouds, he could not rely on his vision. Squeezing his eyes tightly shut, he focused his mind to the path ahead. Finding it clear, he attempted to move his thoughts toward the trees, but he could not hold the spell. "I don't see anything on the road," he said, slightly defeated.

"They're there," Nera replied. "I can't see them anymore, but I can hear them whispering. They're watching the road. I don't think it's safe to go on."

"What do we do?" Kwil asked. Going into the forest at night was dangerous. He preferred to stay close to the road.

"I'm not sure," Nera said, looking toward the trees on the opposite side of the road from the men. She didn't want to be in the woods any more than her companion did, but they had limited options. With a sigh, she said, "We don't have much choice."

"We could stay here awhile," he suggested.

Nera didn't like that suggestion either. Time was not on their side. They needed to make it to Rili's house before anyone could figure out where they were going. The snap of a twig caught her attention, her ears turning themselves toward the noise. From the darkness, a firm hand grasped her shoulder, and she tumbled to the ground.

"Nera!" Kwil cried, taking a step forward. The rough grip of a stranger, his fingers clasped against Kwil's cloak, held him in place.

Three men surrounded the pair, all of them dressed in black, their catlike eyes gleaming in the darkness. "You two are up past your bedtime," one of them said, laughing. Flashing his yellowed fangs, he added, "I'll be relieving you of your money and jewelry."

Nera rose to her knees and said, "We don't have any money." The statement was only partly true. She had brought enough to purchase food and necessities, but she didn't have any to spare.

"A woman who dresses her slave in such a fine cloak has far more money than sense," the brigand replied, gripping the back of Kwil's neck. "Hand it over, and no one gets hurt."

"I don't know about that, Boss," one of the shadowy figures said. "I'd like to have a go at that girl. She's a sweet one." Audibly licking his lips, the Gatan focused his gaze on Nera.

Kwil, who had stood frozen throughout the encounter, knew he had to do something. Though a slave would be executed for attacking a Gatan, he had to protect his friend. Reaching deep into his magical stores, he summoned a fire in his belly. The heat rose through his body, seeping through his skin. The thug's eyes nearly bulged out of his head as he felt the heat against his hand. Smoke arose between the two, his companions staring in disbelief.

Nera took advantage of the distraction and grabbed a hefty branch from the ground. Swinging it with all her might, she connected with the nearest brigand's skull. He dropped to the ground unconscious. Swinging at the second man, she slammed the branch into his midsection, and he doubled over, clutching at his ribs.

The third bandit grabbed for Nera, knocking her to the ground and wrestling the branch from her hands. Kwil took a deep breath and focused his mind to the flames inside. Though he did not know the proper spell for such magic, he willed the heat to obey him. It flew from his fingertips, lighting the brigand's fur ablaze. The man thrashed on the ground, desperately trying to extinguish the flames.

Nera hopped up from the ground and grabbed Kwil by the arm. "Let's go!" she shouted. The two flew toward the forest, disappearing within the black.

Chapter 7

Stumbling through the darkened forest, Kwil did his best to keep stride with his nimble companion. The pair ran a few miles before stopping to catch their breath. Nera leaned forward, her hands against her knees, while Kwil constantly turned his head, searching the night for every sound that crept into his ears.

"It's all right," Nera reassured him. "I don't hear or see any sign of those men." Coming to his side she patted him on the back. "Good job back there."

Shaking his head, Kwil still couldn't believe what he'd managed to do. "I took one of the spells I learned that was designed for lighting candles," he said. "It shouldn't have produced enough heat to do that."

"Well, whatever you did, it worked like a charm," she said. "Those guys didn't know what hit them." She slapped his back once more before plopping herself on the ground. "How about lighting us a fire?"

Kneeling next to her, he replied, "Are you sure that's a good idea? They might see it and come back."

"True, but it's getting really cold, and we don't want to freeze. If someone finds us huddled together, things could get ugly fast." Scanning the ground for rocks or twigs, she fashioned a neat pile for her companion to light.

"Maybe I can camouflage the fire," he said, steadying himself and closing his eyes. Pulling magic through his body, he summoned the same heat he had tapped into before. Placing his hands on one of the rocks, he transferred the heat onto its cold surface. The rock began to heat, its surface taking on an orange glow. Soon, a fire roared to life, spreading to the other rocks and sticks. The magical flame did not consume the wood. Instead, the objects held the flame, preventing it from spreading into the forest.

Sitting back on his heels, Kwil finally opened his eyes. The glow was almost hypnotic, allowing him to enter a trancelike state. Focusing his mind to create colors, he summoned dark blue, green, and brown to cover the burning embers. Those passing by would see nothing of the fire—only Kwil could detect it beneath the illusion he created.

"Good job," Nera said, beaming with pride. "I couldn't have done that."

"You could if you tried harder," he replied, taking his blanket from his bag. Wrapping it around his shoulders, he moved closer to the fire's warmth.

Nera placed her blanket on her lap and reached for her lute case. Examining the instrument, she said, "At least this wasn't damaged when that jerk knocked me down." Pulling the lute from its case, she strummed softly to the night until her fingers were too fatigued to continue.

Lulled by a symphony of nocturnal creatures, the two eventually drifted off to sleep. By the time dawn broke, they awoke refreshed in their forest cradles. Nera leaned up on an arm and took in her surroundings. The road was not in sight, and she wasn't sure which direction they had come.

Rising to her feet, she asked, "Which way is it to the road?"

Kwil stood and observed the ground. "I don't see our footprints," he said. A blanket of fallen leaves masked any sign of their approach. Only an experienced tracker could have found them, and neither of the two had any such skill.

"I'll just have to climb one of these trees and have a look," Nera decided, looking up at the treetops. Finding one with suitably placed branches, she pulled herself upward.

"Are you sure this is wise?" Kwil asked, his voice shaking slightly. "You could fall."

"Nonsense," she replied. "I've been climbing trees since I was a kit."

Kwil wanted to remind her she was no longer a kit. She was a grown, noble lady, and climbing trees was dangerous. But there was no stopping Nera once her mind was made up. All he could do was watch as she moved higher through the branches. Holding his breath, he awaited the sound of her voice.

Placing each hand with care, Nera made sure to keep three points of contact at all times. The bark was damp from the previous day's rain, and she regretted not removing her shoes before beginning her climb. Her footpads would have provided more grip against the slick surface. Carefully digging her claws into the bark, she moved methodically toward the top.

Scanning the treetops, she easily spotted the road. Calling down to Kwil, she said, "I see it! It's southwest of here, maybe three miles away."

Swiveling his head toward the rising sun, Kwil determined which direction they needed to walk. "All right," he called back to her. "You can come down now."

Beginning her descent, Nera neglected to properly secure her feet before moving her arm. Her shoes slipped against the wet bark, her hand desperately reaching for the branch above her. Despite stretching as far as she could, her fingers proved too short. Her body came away from the trunk, narrowly missing the branch below her. Realizing she was falling, she cried out.

Hearing her scream, Kwil jerked his head in time to see her plummet past a second branch. Summoning his magic, he blasted a beam of white light toward her, stopping her in midair. Holding her securely in place, he took a deep breath and focused his energy to holding the spell.

"Thanks for saving me from breaking my neck," Nera said, hovering several feet above the ground. Unsure why she was still hanging in the air, she added, "You can lower me down now."

"I don't know how," Kwil admitted, swallowing hard. Having never manipulated an object weighing more than a few pounds, he was unsure how to proceed with Nera. If he moved her too fast, he risked losing control and dropping her.

This was not the time for her friend to have so much self-doubt. "You can do this, Kwil," Nera said. "I trust you." She held her breath, bracing herself just in case.

With his friend's words of encouragement echoing in his ears, the young mage attempted to calm his mind. Blocking out the rest of the world, he carefully moved his fingers, creating the gentlest path of descent he could manage. Nera drifted softly to the ground.

Lying flat on her back, Nera finally let out the breath she had been holding. Sitting up, she said, "Nice job. Maybe we can practice righting a person so they land on their feet."

Kwil nodded and began to laugh. Soon, both friends were laughing as they collected their blankets and extinguished the fire. Within minutes they were on their way back to the road, the fallen leaves crunching beneath their feet.

"I'm kind of hungry," Nera said. "Let's get something to eat as soon as we reach the town."

Kwil agreed. There wasn't much left to forage in these woods, thanks to the hand of winter. They pressed on, their stomachs rumbling. Only one rider passed them on the road, and he took no notice of the pair. Soon they could hear the sounds of a town nearby, and their hearts lifted at the thought of a warm meal.

Entering the town, they found it bustling with activity. Hundreds of people moved about the various shops, some of them looking to buy, others looking to barter. They pulled carts behind them and held bundles under their arms, all of them moving with purpose as if there were no time to spare. One man led a herd of sheep through town, calling out to potential customers as he went.

"I smell fresh bread," Nera said, her nose held high in the air. Stopping outside a small tavern, she said, "Let's eat here."

Kwil's eyes darted nervously. "I don't think slaves are allowed to eat inside," he said. "Usually, we would pick up our master's order at the back door."

Frowning, Nera replied, "You're my guest. If I invite you inside, that's my own business."

"That isn't how it works, Nera," he replied. "I'm still a slave to these people. Taking me inside will only lead to trouble."

"Fine," Nera said. "Find us someplace out here to sit, and I'll go inside and fetch the food."

With a nod, Kwil moved around to the back of the tavern, his eyes searching for a suitable place to eat. A large oak tree stood out of the way of the hustle and bustle. Choosing the side facing away from the road, he sat with his hands on his knees, awaiting Nera's return.

It wasn't long before she reappeared, two small bundles held in her hands. Spotting Kwil beneath the tree, she made her way over and handed him some food. "Pot roast," she announced. "With carrots, and apple pie for dessert."

Gratefully taking the bundle, Kwil tried to remember if he'd ever tasted apple pie. He had not. The scent of the meal was intoxicating, and he closed his eyes for a moment to savor it. A massive hunk of bread, covered with butter and honey, was included in his bundle. Holding it up, he said, "This is big enough to be a meal itself."

Nodding, Nera said, "It won't keep on the road, so eat as much as you can."

Kwil obeyed. Surprising himself, he put away every bite of his meal, including the extra-large helping of pie. It was the best thing he'd ever tasted. "Why don't they serve this at the College?" he wondered.

"They like to keep us on a strict diet," Nera replied. "Healthy food only." Wiping her hands on her pant legs, she said, "Ready to find Master Rili? He shouldn't be far from here."

Hopping up, Kwil asked, "You don't know exactly where he lives?"

"No, but I could ask around," she replied. "I'm sure it isn't far from here."

"We should probably try finding him on our own first," he suggested. "We don't want to draw attention to ourselves. Someone might be looking for us."

"Good point," Nera replied.

Together they walked back to the road, pausing momentarily beside the tavern. "Are you sure you don't want more of that pie for the trip?" Kwil asked, grinning.

Laughing, Nera replied, "I think I've had enough. Let's see if we can't find Rili. Maybe he can teach you how to conjure more desserts."

They headed through the town, intending to scour the countryside for paths that might lead to Rili's house. As they passed a well-dressed man, he cried out unexpectedly.

"Your slave bumped into me!" he shouted, pointing at Kwil.

Nera stopped dead in her tracks. "No he didn't," she argued.

"How dare you, woman?" the man replied, his face reddening.

"Listen—" she started to say. A sharp look from Kwil convinced her to hold her tongue. When others were around, she had to be his master, not his friend. With a sigh, she asked, "Slave, did you bump into this man?"

Kwil shook his head but did not speak.

"You would call me a liar?" the man replied, stepping forward. By this time, a crowd had gathered behind him, eager to see what had caused the disturbance. Many of them voiced their displeasure at Kwil's response.

"He said he didn't do it," Nera said, grabbing Kwil by the arm. She could tell the crowd was turning ugly, and they needed to get out of town quickly. "We'll be on our way," she said, turning around.

The man stepped forward, grabbing Kwil's other arm and violently dragging him to the ground. The mage did not resist. Harming a noble, especially with witnesses, would put his life in danger.

"Not until this one has been punished for his insolence!" the man shouted. The crowd shouted their approval as a small child ran up to kick Kwil in the ribs as he lay on the ground. Nera started forward, but another man grabbed her.

"You stay out of this, Miss," he said, his expression severe.

Nera struggled momentarily, but stopped when she saw the city guards approaching.

"What's the problem here?" one guard asked.

"This slave ran into me," the nobleman explained. "Then he called me a liar."

"He didn't!" Nera shouted.

"Is this your slave?" the guard asked.

"He is," she replied. The man who was holding her finally loosened his grip, allowing her to speak freely to the guards. "He is innocent of this crime," she declared. "I was with him the entire time. Let us leave, and we won't return."

The guard grinned. "You can do just that—after we teach him some manners."

Nera stood frozen in place. As she watched in horror, the second guard knelt and tied Kwil's hands behind his back. Kicking him twice, he shouted at the slave to stand. As soon as the young man obeyed, the guard reached for the leather whip attached to his belt. With a smooth stroke, he struck Kwil's back with the lash, a bright line of blood appearing on his white shirt.

Nera tried to shove her way through the crowd, but the onlookers had formed a tight circle around her friend. She could not push her way through. All she could do was shout, her cries going unheard over the cacophony of voices. Turning her face away, she did not see the second or third lash her friend received, but the crack of the whip echoed in her ears, and she cringed with each blow.

"That's enough," the first guard said. "Show's over! Everyone back to your business!"

The crowd gave no argument. Satisfied with the human's blood, they moved away, leaving him on his knees. Nera rushed forward, taking his head in her arms.

"Are you all right?" she asked.

He nodded, his eyes still wide with fear. Taking her arm, he pulled himself to his feet.

"We need to clean your wounds," Nera said.

Shaking his head, Kwil whispered, "Wait until we're out of town."

Though his skin tightened and stung with every step, Kwil made it out of town quickly, never letting go of Nera's arm. They made their way to the trees to avoid any citizens who might be watching. Nera helped Kwil to sit and removed the shredded shirt from his back.

Pulling a handkerchief from her pack, she applied pressure to the deepest slash. The mage winced slightly at her touch, but settled down after a few seconds.

"You should have used your magic," Nera scolded. "You could have blasted that lying bastard into pieces."

"We both would have been punished if I had used magic," he replied, his throat raspy.

"You could have kept throwing fire at them until they stopped following us," she replied. "They deserved it, the way they stood there cheering." Her teeth clenched as she remembered the cries of the crowd, encouraging the guards to strike harder. Even the children had joined in. Such cruelty was unacceptable in a civilized society. How could so many stand by while an innocent man was treated that way?

"I'm not skilled enough to take on a whole town," Kwil said. "And even if I were, I wouldn't want to hurt them." He laughed softly, doing his best to ignore the searing pain. "If I'd known how to disappear, that would have been helpful."

"You shouldn't have to disappear," she argued. "There should be justice in this land, and no one should have to be treated that way." She was furious, and she planned to keep the image of her injured friend in her mind for the rest of her days. Something had to be done about this. "Slavery and inequality can't be allowed to continue. I'm going to put a stop to it someday."

Though he appreciated his friend's dedication, he knew such a thing was impossible. "One person can't change the world, Nera."

Staring at the bloody handkerchief in her hand, she replied, "One can try."

Chapter 8

"Do you know a spell that will help this heal faster?" Nera asked, staring at the dried blood on her friend's back.

Shaking his head, Kwil replied, "Those spells are for advanced students. You might have learned them in your fourth year."

"I never would have made it that far," she replied, sighing. Though she wanted to hurry in finding Rili, she knew Kwil needed to rest. Every time he moved, the scabs would open up, and the bleeding would start all over. If only she had some practical skills, she might know how to stitch the wounds. Instead, she had learned nothing useful in all her studies. Only poor children learned how to do such things. As a noble, she was expected to hire out any job that required any work. Ladies were expected to sit around and be waited upon and nothing more.

With little else to be done, she sat back on the ground and ran her hand along the smooth wood of her lute case. "I guess we'll have to avoid everyone we see from now on," she remarked, flipping the case open and staring at her lute.

In a gentle tone, Kwil asked, "Are you angry with me?"

Sighing, she replied, "No, I'm angry at the world, my father, and my entire race for allowing slavery to continue." She paused a moment before asking, "Why don't the slaves revolt?"

With a shrug, he replied, "There just aren't enough of us I guess. I don't usually encounter more than one or two working for any given family." Considering his own luck at being taught to read, he added, "And it's hard for people with no education, no weapons or training, and nowhere to go to decide it's time to fight."

"I would fight," Nera declared, still staring at her lute.

"Maybe some of us aren't treated as bad as others. My situation could be worse."

Looking up at him, she asked, "So you just accept it?" She shook her head. "I couldn't."

"You'd be surprised what you'd be willing to do to survive," he replied. "If I angered your father, he could have me locked away forever, or worse, kill me. I'd never see the sky again, and I wouldn't learn any more magic. Look at what I'd have missed out on if I'd rebelled against him. We wouldn't be friends." He hoped those words would bring a smile to her face, but they did not. "There's a lot I haven't done, and I'm not ready to stop dreaming that I might actually do some of it someday."

Her demeanor softening, Nera tried her best to understand. There were worse fates than death, and slavery was probably one of them. "I am glad to have you as a friend, Kwil," she stated. "I just wish we had met under different circumstances."

"If I'd been born a Gatan," he replied with a smile.

"Yes," she replied. "Or if I'd been born a human." Finally taking the lute from its case, she gently stroked the polished wood. "Tell me about your family," she said. "Where are your parents?"

"I don't remember them," he admitted. "But sometimes I dream of a woman who sings to me. I think she might be my mother, but I can't be sure."

After a pause, he added, "I usually dream about her when I'm feeling low."

"She brings you comfort," Nera said. "I bet she is your mother. You're remembering her from when you were a baby."

"No one can remember his first year of life," he replied dismissively. He felt a little embarrassed at having mentioned the dreams.

"No normal person," Nera said. "But you aren't normal. You have a natural talent for magic, and it wouldn't surprise me if it was magic that made you remember her. Maybe she has magic too, and she sends you those dreams to let you know she loves you."

The thought gave him pause. Maybe his mother really was communicating with him. It was certainly better than the alternative—that she was a slave stuck in the service of a breeder and living a life of misery. He pictured the golden-haired woman standing tall and proud, surrounded by the glow of white magic. He couldn't stop himself from smiling.

Nera took notice of his expression and laughed. "It's good to see you can still smile after all that's happened," she said. "Tell you what. After we've had you trained as a master wizard, I'll help you look for her." After a moment, she added, "If you want me to, that is."

"I'd like that," he replied, still beaming.

* * * * *

After an uneventful night of rest, Kwil awoke feeling refreshed. He pulled a new shirt over his head before fastening his cloak.

Nera grinned. "It looks great on you." The shirt's fabric was dark green and thick enough to keep out the chill. Had he not been human, her friend's clothing would have given the impression he was a nobleman. The way he carried himself, though, was unusual for someone of the upper class. "You shouldn't slouch so much," she scolded. "Stand up tall, and keep your head high. Master Rili will take you more seriously if he thinks you're sure of your abilities."

"I'll try," he promised.

Nera planned to make sure he kept his word. If ever he appeared to be faltering, she would be there to remind him. He was no longer a slave, even if no other Gatan was willing to accept it. He was a free man.

A gentle snow began to fall as the two prepared to begin their search for Master Rili's home. Luckily the

109

wind stayed light, and the snow was powdery instead of ice.

"Should we get back on the road?" Kwil asked. "If the snow gets heavier, we might lose our way in the forest."

Glancing toward the road, Nera said, "Let's stay here for now. We can keep the road in sight and move over if the snow starts getting deep." Staying safe was more important to her than following the road, but the snow would likely keep other travelers at home. The road might be safer than she thought.

For nearly an hour they traveled through the forest. Thankfully the snow remained light, and they moved with surprising ease. Unfortunately, there was no sign of Rili's home or any type of path that might lead them to it.

"Maybe we should try the other side of the road," Kwil suggested.

"Agreed," Nera replied. They had already gone farther from town than she had anticipated. They should have seen some sign of Rili by now, assuming the rumors she had heard about him were true. Crossing the road seemed a better idea than climbing another tree for a look around. She wasn't sure she wanted to take the risk of falling while Kwil was not at a hundred percent. His poor treatment at the hands of the town's citizens might have temporarily affected his magical abilities.

With caution they approached the road, looking each way before darting across. No one saw them, save the ever-watching eyes of a single owl. They pressed on through the woods, directing their footsteps back in the direction of the town.

An object darted past Kwil, his eyes catching only the slightest glimpse. "Was that a hummingbird?" he wondered. The strange creature made a loud buzzing sound, but it was too cold for most insects to be active.

Not having seen the winged being, Nera replied, "It's winter. The hummingbirds have all gone."

"Something flew past my head," he stated.

"It was probably just a leaf," she replied. Normally, she wouldn't give the matter a second thought, but the buzzing returned, this time beside her own head. As the noise grew more intense, she turned to find a black-and-white furry creature hovering just behind her. It was about three inches long with insectlike wings and a long, protruding stinger on its abdomen. "Ahh!" she screamed, flailing her hands to swat the beast away.

Kwil looked over at his companion, neglecting where his feet were about to step. His boot landed near the roots of an aging pine, where the menacing creatures made their nest. A swarm of furry fliers emerged, surrounding the hapless travelers. Kwil waved his arms, hoping to deter the beasts from such large prey, but it was no use. One of them plunged its stinger into his arm, the sensation of fire spreading throughout his body.

"Run!" Nera shouted, bounding away from the nest. Both of them darted through the underbrush, ignoring any obstacles in their path. All that mattered was outrunning the stinging monsters.

The buzzing devils pursued, matching pace with the two hapless wanderers. Determination gleaming in their coal-black eyes, they charged on, occasionally lunging their stingers toward the pair. One managed to make contact with Nera's cloak, but the wool was too thick to allow the stinger to penetrate. The creature worked itself free and continued its pursuit.

Shoving past low branches and leaping over roots, Kwil and Nera pressed on. Their hearts pounding and their lungs screaming for them to stop, they ran, fueled only by adrenaline. Kwil's arm throbbed where the stinger had landed, and a large purple welt formed on his skin. Ignoring the pain, he ran on, barely able to keep pace with his nimble companion.

Nera leapt higher with each passing root, swatting her hands in the air the entire time. Though she was well ahead of the buzzers for the time being, she believed she could feel them brushing against her fur. Only the sound of Kwil's footsteps behind her let her know he was still keeping pace. Hoping his awkward human legs would not fail him, she continued her flight.

"Water!" Kwil cried, pointing to the right. A large pond remained unfrozen, its ice-cold waters far more inviting than the stingers.

The two rushed toward the shore, slipping on the dampened leaves that surrounded it. Kwil did not hesitate to jump, landing feet-first in the frigid water. Nera paused, her eyes wide. Placing her foot in the water up to the ankle, she felt hundreds of needles piercing her skin. Wondering whether she should take her chances with the angry fliers, she withdrew her foot and shivered.

"Come on!" Kwil shouted. "They're still coming!" The beasts had no trouble catching up to the Gatan, and her only choice was to join her companion in the water.

Looking over her shoulder, Nera's fear of the buzzers renewed. Taking in a deep breath, she jumped into the icy water. Submerged to her neck, she felt safe from the stingers, but her breath was stolen away. Thankfully, the monsters preferred not to follow. For them, becoming wet meant they could not fly, and that meant certain death. They buzzed away, content that the intruders were far from their nest.

Shivering, the pair made their way to the bank and climbed out onto dry land. Kwil made it out with little trouble, but Nera's soaked fur made her heavy. Her hands grasped at the ground, trying to pull her freezing body from the water. Kwil grabbed onto her arms and pulled, nearly dragging her out of the lake. Her teeth chattered, and ice crystals formed on her exposed fur.

"You have to build a fire," she squeaked out.

Nodding, Kwil gathered a sloppy pile of fallen leaves and held his hand above it. Trying his best to focus his mind, he reached for the heat inside himself. Nothing happened. Opening his eyes was difficult. They felt like they were frozen shut. "I'm too cold!" he said, panicking. Both of their lives depended on his ability to cast this spell, and he was failing.

Nera managed to move her freezing body to his side and came to her knees. Grabbing his hands, she squeezed them tightly. "Use my energy," she suggested.

Though he'd never tried to pull energy from another creature, Kwil had read it was possible. Clearing his mind of thoughts of cold, he attempted to tap into Nera's heat. He found none. She was colder than he was, and he could find no warmth inside her to project into the fire. "It's not working," he said, his voice barely more than a whisper.

Nera let go of his hands and placed both of hers against his face. Looking into his eyes, she said, "You can do this, Kwil. I believe in you."

Trying again, Kwil found it impossible to calm his mind. He was too cold, and felt only the desire to lie down and rest. But a fire burned in Nera's eyes. Determined not to let her down, he reached out instinctively, placing his hands against the sides of her head. Placing his forehead against hers he drew not heat but confidence. His mind began to clear, thoughts of cold and death disappearing into the frigid, winter air. Summoning the heat inside his gut, he forced it up through his hand. Gesturing to the leaf pile, he projected the fire, red magic erupting from his fingertips. An ember glowed to life within the leaves, its life-giving warmth caressing the frozen travelers.

"You did it!" Nera cried, clapping her hands. As the words escaped her lips, Kwil collapsed, teetering over onto his side. "You can't sleep now," she said, shaking her head. Grabbing him by his shoulders, she shook him violently.

His eyes opened, and he steadied himself before the fire. Nera began disrobing, eager to get the wet clothes away from her fur. Kwil turned his head to allow the woman her modesty.

Slinging her cloak over a limb, she said, "Don't worry about that now. You should get those wet clothes hung up over the fire too." Grinning, she added, "Before they stick to your pink skin." After stripping down to her undergarments, she sat cross-legged on the ground, rubbing her arms and legs.

Rising to his feet, Kwil removed his cloak and shirt, but wouldn't go so far as to remove his pants. There was a lady present, after all. The fire's warmth found its way to his bare skin, soothing the tightness that had crept into his muscles. His magical energy renewed, he decided to augment the fire. Placing his hand over the top, he projected more heat, increasing the output of the flames. Though it appeared unchanged, the increase in warmth caused their icy clothes to steam.

"Nice," Nera commented, watching. "We'll be dry in no time."

"That was the plan," Kwil replied with a smile. His confidence heightened, he was eager to get dry and go looking for Master Rili. His future lay somewhere in these woods, and he was ready to find it.

Chapter 9

After returning to the road, it wasn't long before Nera spotted a worn path, partially concealed by layers of dried leaves. Pointing, she shouted, "Look! That must be the way!"

The pair broke into a run, anxious to finally meet the master wizard who they hoped would take them in. Winding along the narrow path, they finally spotted a manor house nestled in the distance.

Kwil paused. "I thought you said he was a poor man." Judging by the size of his home, Kwil couldn't believe that rumor had been true.

"I guess he isn't anymore," Nera replied, staring at the house. It was smaller than her own family's home, but sufficiently large to mark the wizard as well off. A large garden jutted off to the side, but luckily, she spotted no slaves tending it. "Come on," she said. They'd come this far, and she was eager to speak to Rili, regardless of his wealth. "Master wizards are probably paid quite nicely," she suggested.

Kwil did not reply but followed his friend up the path to the manor.

Arriving at the door Nera said, "Let me do the talking."

Having no intention of addressing the wizard without permission, Kwil happily allowed her to speak on his behalf. He stood behind her and slightly to the side, hoping to avoid notice.

Knocking loudly upon the wooden door, Nera announced her presence at the manor. Doing her best to appear refined, she straightened her back and held her head high. To her surprise, Master Rili himself answered the door in lieu of a servant. His hooded cloak and sparkling green eyes gave him away instantly. With the unmistakable air of a master wizard, his black-and-white fur radiated magic.

"Yes?" Rili looked her up and down. He did not spare a glance at Kwil.

Clearing her throat, Nera said, "I have come seeking your instruction, Master."

Rili scoffed. "I'm afraid you're out of luck. The College is that way." He pointed a well-manicured finger in the direction of the road and slowly pushed the door to close it. Nera's foot stopped him. Scowling, he asked, "Is there something else?"

"Please," she began, "I can't go back to the College. You're the only person who will understand my predicament. May we come in?"

At the word "we," Rili glanced over at the slave standing silently near one of the marble columns decorating the front of the manor. "You and your slave?" he asked, curious.

"Yes," she replied. "I must speak with you. It's a matter of life or death." She hoped those words would gain her entry into the master's home. Outside she felt too exposed to reveal her secret.

Pushing the door aside, Rili sighed. "Come in, I suppose." Moving aside, he observed carefully as Nera and Kwil stepped inside. Gesturing to Nera, he said, "Have a seat."

Moving to a velvet-covered chair, Nera made herself comfortable. Kwil took a position behind her, standing at the ready as a slave was expected to do.

Taking a seat across from his guests, Rili asked, "Now what is this urgent life or death business?" The two were certainly an unusual arrival to his home. Visitors were extremely rare, save those who came to deliver supplies. The wizard preferred his solitude in order to focus on his work.

Nera wasn't sure where to begin, but she knew she had to tell the truth. There would be no keeping secrets from this man. Trust was key—without it she couldn't know that Kwil would be safe. It was best to know where Rili stood right away, in case they needed to make another escape. "I," she started, "we, would like to study magic with you."

Rili stared blankly at the girl. "Who's we?" he asked. She couldn't possibly be referring to herself and the slave. She must have some other person in mind.

Raising her hand, she patted Kwil's arm. "This is Kwil, and I am Nera. We are both interested in learning magic." Though she wasn't truly interested for herself, she thought it might increase Kwil's chances if she was learning too. If Rili thought he would be spending too much one-on-one time with a human, he might not be so keen on the idea. Once he saw that Kwil was progressing far beyond Nera's abilities, Rili would hopefully warm to the idea.

Jumping to his feet, Rili stammered a moment before asking, "A slave? You want me to train your slave?" The entire notion was ludicrous. He had already spent a small fortune aiding runaway slaves by funding their departure on trustworthy ships. The work was dangerous, and the few ships' captains willing to take on such an endeavor demanded a hefty sum. Rili did not agree with Gi'gata's attitude toward slavery, but taking one into his home would be madness.

"Please hear me out," Nera said in a calm tone. To her surprise, Rili relaxed a bit and sat back down. "Until a few days ago, I was a second year student at the College," she explained. "Kwil was my servant. He learned from my books, and he has a natural talent for magic. I made the mistake of asking one of my teachers to help him. She wanted to have him killed."

"I'm not surprised," Rili responded. "You would likely be imprisoned as well." After a pause, he said, "You're asking me to shelter two criminals and contribute to their crime." He shook his head, trying to figure out why they'd come to him. Most people left him in peace, and he preferred it that way. His upbringing and training as a sorcerer had not been easy, thanks to his low birth. He had to fight for everything he accomplished, and now these two strangers had arrived and asked him to risk losing everything. Being involved in this criminal act could cost him his freedom, or possibly his life.

"We wouldn't be here if we had anywhere else to go," Nera went on. "I've heard about you, your past difficulties, and that you were sympathetic toward slaves." Staring into his eyes, she could not tell whether she was reaching him at all. "Kwil, show him what you can do."

Hesitating a moment, Kwil decided it was for the best. Rili didn't seem eager to take him on as a student, so he had to prove he was worth the effort. Reaching into his magic, he whispered an incantation and waved his fingers in a precise motion. Five books removed themselves from the shelf behind Rili, shuffled three times, and took their rightful places back on the shelf. Finishing the spell, Kwil's eyes darted between Nera and Rili.

Nera pleaded, "He deserves to learn. Please, Sir."

Still staring at the books, Rili turned slowly back toward his guests. His eyes fell on Kwil, and he shook his head. "In all my studies I've never encountered a human wizard." Pausing, he rubbed a finger against his chin. To Nera, he said, "We are an egotistical bunch, we Gatans. We assume that the races of other lands are inferior, but that isn't the case. Wherever this young man is from, his people obviously practice magic. Our people declare it impossible because we wish it were so."

"Does that mean you'll teach him?" Nera asked, trying to quell the excitement in her voice.

"Him?" he asked. "I thought you wanted to learn as well." Now he understood. She was here only to help her friend.

Nera bowed her head. "I have no talent for magic," she admitted. "Kwil is the one who really needs you."

"All Gatans are capable of magic," Rili replied. "If you have no desire to hone the skill, I will not force you. But Kwil must prove himself a worthy student. Simply shuffling books isn't good enough. He must prove he has the ability to think—to find solutions to impossible tasks. Only then will I agree to teach him."

"I will take any test you give me," Kwil stated boldly. "Please, name the task, and I will find a way to carry it out."

Rili admired the slave's dedication. He was eager to learn, and that made him worthy of a chance. Despite never having taken on an apprentice before, Rili considered himself up to the challenge. It didn't take long for him to decide on an appropriate test of Kwil's cunning. "You must draw water from the well out back without using any type of bowl or cup. Bring the water inside to me, and I will determine if you are a worthy student."

Motioning for them to follow, Rili led his guests toward the rear of the manor and opened the door to the garden. Silently he watched as the two filed out in the cold. Shutting the door behind him, he went back inside to sit by the fire.

"He's not going to watch?" Nera asked. She expected him to stand over Kwil's shoulder and scrutinize his every move.

With a shrug, Kwil replied, "It doesn't matter. He'll know." Approaching the well, Kwil peered inside. A single bucket attached to a rope descended into the depths. "It's an ordinary well," he declared. Now the question was which spell to choose.

"Can you use the same spell you used on the books?" Nera asked. As soon as she said it, she knew it was the wrong answer. Rili would never make it that easy.

"I'd have to control each molecule of water individually, since it doesn't stick together the way a solid object does," Kwil explained. No, there was another solution. All he had to do was find it.

Nera moved toward the well and sat on its edge. Preparing to swing her feet around, she said, "Lower me down like you did when I fell out of the tree. I'll cup it in my hands." A proud smile graced her lips, satisfied with her own cunning.

Kwil shook his head. "It will leak through your fingers. There won't be any left by the time we reach the door."

"Then I'll get a mouthful," she said, dangling her feet over the well's edge.

"I can't risk lowering you in there, Nera," Kwil said. "Not without Rili here to save you if I fail."

Waving her hand, she dismissed the comment. "You can do it. I trust you."

"This isn't about trust," he replied. "You could drown, and I won't risk it." Looking at her with a sparkle in his eye, he said, "Ask me again when I'm a master wizard."

Laughing, Nera hopped down from the well's edge and stood beside her friend. He had an idea, and she was anxious to see what it was.

Knowing how well he had done with the heat spell, Kwil focused his mind to heating the water. Beads of sweat formed on his forehead as he continued to pour heat into the well, the water beneath bubbling in response. Concentrating intently on the task at hand, he neglected to blink his eyes or let out the breath he was holding. He teetered slightly, but Nera lent a hand to steady him. Without losing his concentration, he took a deep breath and pulled the steam up from the water's surface.

Nera clapped her hands as a cloud of water vapor formed itself into a sphere and hovered above her friend's upturned palm. "You did it!" she shouted.

"Not yet," Kwil said. "I have to get it back to Master Rili." Fearing he might lose control of the vapor, he paused for a moment, standing perfectly still. Putting more concentration into the spell than necessary, he felt himself waning. He had to remain strong if he was going to succeed.

As if reading his mind, Nera said, "You're doing great, Kwil. This is the easy part."

She was correct. Heating the water and carrying it was easier than what came next. He had to correctly perform the spell that would turn the evaporated water back to liquid, and he wasn't sure he could do it. Taking great care with each step, he moved at a snail's pace toward the manor door. Nera rushed in front of him to open it, and he stepped inside, barely able to contain his excitement. Only a few moments more of concentration, and he would prove to Rili he was a worthy student.

Hearing their footsteps, Rili rose from his seat and joined them as they moved into the dining room. Seeing the cloud of water vapor in Kwil's hand, he raised his eyebrows but said nothing.

Willing the water vapor to float toward a wooden bowl on the table, Kwil continued to focus his mind. His heart rate spiked, and his breathing became heavier as the water hovered above its target. Closing his eyes and hoping for the best, he muttered a quiet incantation. Stumbling on his words, he paused and cleared his throat. Trying again, he spoke slower, enunciating the words through a shaky voice. Drawing the heat away from the vapor, he allowed it to cool to its former state. As his eyes opened, the vapor liquefied, pouring itself into the bowl. An immense feeling of relief swept over him. The spell had actually worked as he had planned. Beaming with pride, he turned to the master wizard for approval.

Narrowing his eyes, Rili inspected the young man closely. "This was your idea?" he asked. "The girl didn't help you?"

Kwil shook his head. "She offered, but I declined," he replied.

"Boiling the water was his idea," Nera stated. "I only thought of carrying it in my hands or mouth."

Rolling his eyes at her silly suggestions, Rili decided she had nothing to do with Kwil's clever trick. The boy had talent, and he had an analytical mind that would serve him well as a student of magic. Rili was pleased. "You've done well," he said to Kwil. "Now you're ready for your second test."

Kwil's heart sank to his feet. He should have known something so simple wouldn't be enough proof. "Name it," he said, ready to accept the challenge.

"You must fetch me the claw of a cockatrice."

Chapter 10

"He'll be killed!" Nera shouted in protest. "It's not a fair test!"

"That is the test he must take," Rili replied calmly.

"I'll do it," Kwil said. Wrinkling his brow, he asked, "What's a cockatrice?"

"Kwil, you can't do this," Nera warned. "A cockatrice is extremely dangerous. It will kill you without a second thought." Turning to Rili, she said, "You can't be serious about this. He isn't ready! A master wizard can't face down a cockatrice."

"If he cannot do it, I will not teach him," the wizard replied. "If he returns victorious, he will become my apprentice." To Kwil, he cautioned, "Don't bringing me a fake. The claws have specific magical properties, and I'll know easily if you're trying to deceive me."

"I would never do that," Kwil replied.

"And the girl must stay here," Rili added. "No one may assist you in this final test."

"You're intentionally making this difficult for him," Nera accused. "You want him to fail!" The injustice of this test made her angry, and she wasn't afraid to let the wizard know it.

Rili raised a hand to silence her. "Either Kwil will accept the test and pass it or he won't. It makes no difference to me."

"I want to do this," Kwil said, his eyes pleading with Nera to cease her argument. "Where can I find this creature?"

"There is a cave about three miles west of here," Rili explained. "Once you've gone about a mile, you'll notice a narrow trail. It is created by the dragging of the cockatrice's tail. Follow that path, and you will see a rock formation when you're about a mile from the cave's entrance. The forest thins out nearer the cave. Good luck to you." Turning his back, he stepped away as carefree as ever.

"You'd think he could be more helpful before he sends a person to his death," Nera commented.

Taking Kwil by the arm, she said, "Listen to me. A cockatrice is part dragon and part bird. Its gaze can turn you to stone, even with the slightest glance. You mustn't look into its eyes."

"I understand," Kwil replied, nodding. "What happens if the creature sees its own gaze?"

"What do you mean?" she asked, puzzled.

"Its reflection," he said. "Like when it takes a drink and sees itself in the water."

"I have no idea," Nera admitted. All she knew was what she'd heard in old legends, and she was barely paying attention. Her mind was always filled with music, and learning about the various monsters in the world held little appeal unless it was told in song.

"Has anyone ever managed this?" Kwil wondered.

Nera could not say. "I hope so," she said. After a pause, she asked, "Are you sure you want to do this?"

Shaking his head, he replied, "I don't want to, Nera, but I have to. Whatever it takes for Master Rili to teach me is what I'm going to do." Leaning forward, he hugged his friend tightly. "This is my dream," he said. "If I don't try, then I'll never be more than a slave."

Feeling the tears welling in her eyes, Nera did her best to hide them. She understood the yearning in his soul. It was the same thing she felt when her father announced she had to become a sorceress when all she ever wanted was to make music. Her dream denied her, she had resigned herself to a life of misery. Meeting Kwil had changed all that. She was now free to create her own future, and so was he. "Go carefully, my friend," she said. "And come back in one piece," she added with a smile.

"I'll do my best," he promised.

Wringing her hands, Nera watched as her friend walked away. He had no weapon with him, and no way to shield himself from the monster's wrath. Rili had sent him completely unprepared, and her heart ached as she watched him walk away. If he didn't return, she would find a way to punish Rili, though she had no idea how to go about facing down a wizard.

Kwil attempted to walk with confidence as he moved away from the manor grounds and into the trees. Was Rili observing him? Would he show up in a flash of light and save Kwil if something went terribly wrong? Shaking his head, Kwil put the thought away. There was little chance the wizard had something like that planned. Maybe he did intend for Kwil to die in this attempt, but if there was a way to succeed, he was determined to find it.

The frozen ground crunching beneath his feet, Kwil pressed on to the west. With each step, he grew more anxious. Taking deep breaths, he did his best to stay calm. After only ten minutes of walking, he felt like he'd been going forever. Glancing back over his shoulder, he could still see the smoke rising from Master Rili's chimney. Determination urged him forward, though his feet felt heavier by the second. This would either be the best day of his life or the last.

When his eye fell on a narrow trail, Kwil's mouth dropped open. This meant he was nearing the cockatrice's cave, and he had better start readying himself in case the creature was skulking about. Every attempt he made to clear his mind failed. His mind raced with visions of vicious claws and flashing scales, and his fear was beginning to take hold.

"You can do this, Kwil," he said out loud. "No point in worrying about it now. You agreed to the task, so do it." Staring up at the sky he focused his mind to the soft gray clouds gathering above him. Nearly becoming dizzy, he stared into the endless void, losing himself inside it. Finally, his mind was calm and clear. With renewed confidence, he continued toward the cave.

Before long, the rock formation Rili had mentioned came into view. It was much larger than Kwil expected, rising high into the sky and spanning several hundred feet across. The stones looked to be etched and possibly shaped by some long-forgotten race of ancients. Heading toward them, the trees thinned out, leaving the young slave exposed. But he did not care. A strange sensation drew him to the rocks. He had to touch them, to feel their smooth stone beneath his fingertips.

As he approached the rocks, he felt magical energy pulsating through his body. Almost too intense at first, he eventually relaxed into the feeling and came to enjoy it. It was revitalizing and energizing, filling his magical stores with a sensation he had never experienced. Was this what it was like to bathe in pure magic? All he knew was, he would gladly stay stuck to this spot forever, absorbing the stones' magic through his veins.

Taking a seat at the base of a tall, pillar-shaped stone, Kwil rested his cheek against its surface. To his delight, the stone was warm, despite winter's chill. It glowed with a pale yellow light, and he raised his hand to shield his eyes. When the light became more intense, he pulled himself away, releasing the bond he had created between himself and the stone. The light faded, leaving him to wonder what had happened.

A flat, round stone lay at his feet, and he decided its smaller size might produce a less dramatic effect. If he could determine what was happening when he touched it, maybe he could learn to use it properly. Placing his palm on the flat surface, he felt the stone's warmth, and the same light began to glow between his fingers. The image of the cockatrice flashed in his mind, and the stone emitted an electric jolt. Pulling his hand away, Kwil tried to shake off the pain. Looking down at the rock, he noticed its surface had been altered—it was now polished to a mirror-like shine.

Looking around, Kwil searched for the source of power at the rocks. He saw nothing besides the plain, gray stones, settled into the frozen ground. If it weren't for the intense feeling of magic in the area, he would never have expected anything to happen.

Was this part of Rili's plan? He had mentioned the rocks after all. Perhaps he knew only a sorcerer would sense the magic in the stones. Kwil wished Nera were here so he could ask if she sensed anything. Her disinterest in magic might make her immune to their effects. If so, Kwil would know that Rili had indeed offered help, though he didn't make it too obvious.

Rising to his feet, Kwil observed his reflection in the rock's surface. Using this against the cockatrice was a far better idea than having it look into water. This was portable and just the right size to serve as a shield. With his heart yearning to study the rock formation further, Kwil knew he had to move on. He wasn't going to find the cockatrice sitting here, and the task was too important to abandon. Hoping that someday Rili would bring him here and explain the magic of the stones, Kwil forced himself to walk away, following along the path carved by the monster's massive form.

As he approached the cave's entrance, fear gripped hold of his mind. No longer certain that he wanted to continue, he hesitated, staring into the mouth of the cave. Only a few feet inside, the light faded away to darkness, and Kwil felt a churning in his stomach. Clutching the polished stone against his chest, he begged it to give him strength. The warmth returned to its surface, spreading throughout the young man's body. Steeling himself, he stepped inside the monster's lair.

To his delight, the shield remained lit, providing enough light for him to easily maneuver through the cave. His feet immediately hit water, and he paused, observing the pool in front of him. It appeared to go down for eternity, its depths descending into blackness. Wondering if he would have to swim across, he became uneasy. Kwil was not the strongest swimmer, but the monster might be. Stooping low, he grabbed a small pebble and tossed it in the water. It splashed, landing no more than a few inches from the water's surface. Looking upward, Kwil realized the pool was only reflecting the darkened ceiling with its partially illuminated stalactites. With a quiet sigh of relief, he continued forward.

A booming voice echoed against the cave walls, startling him to attention. "Who wanders so foolishly into my abode?" the voice asked. The words were followed by audible footsteps—the heavy, resounding steps of a massive beast.

His throat nearly too dry to speak, Kwil did his best to project. "My name is Kwil," he began, "and I've come to ask a favor of you." Civility, he decided, was the best option here. This creature was intelligent enough to speak, so maybe he could reason with it to avoid a fight.

Laughter resounded throughout the cavern. "You are a bold fool," the monster said. "What favor would you ask of me?"

Swallowing hard, he replied, "A single claw is all. My master requires it."

A brief silence followed, and the young man tilted his ear toward the cave's depths. He recognized the faint sound of dragging and the dripping of water, but nothing of the cockatrice's voice. Shining the light of his shield throughout the cavern, he counted no fewer than five passageways. With the echoing sounds, he could never guess which way the voice had come from.

Without warning, a heavy blow knocked him off his feet, his shield scooting away from him along the muddy floor. Its light faded out before Kwil could scramble to his feet.

"I'll be keeping all of my claws today!" the cockatrice roared. With a swipe of its tail, it struck a second time, slamming Kwil against the cave wall.

Pain exploding through his body, Kwil struggled to suck in a breath. Dropping to his knees, he clawed desperately at the floor, searching for the stone shield. Feeling the beast's breath on his neck, Kwil instinctively rolled to the side, narrowly avoiding a gnashing beak. Groping in the darkness, he continued to search for the shield, knowing he must find it or die.

The cockatrice struck again, sending the slave's bruised body sliding into a shallow puddle. As he came to a halt, he flipped himself over and coughed up a mouthful of pebbles and mud. When he reached out his hands to steady himself, his fingers brushed against warmth—he had found the stone. Its light glowed as the mage's hand grasped it, and he lifted it high in the air. With the cavern illuminated, he got his first glimpse of the creature that had attacked him.

Golden scales glittered in the pale light, its long slender neck rising to the height of the cave. A menacing hiss escaped its hooked beak as Kwil trembled at the sight. When the creature spread its batlike wings, the slave pulled the shield close to his head, shielding his eyes from the beast's gaze.

Realizing the intruder carried a polished stone, the cockatrice commended him. "Clever boy!" it shouted. "You've come prepared!" In a fluid motion, it swung its spiny tail, and sent the mage flying.

Biting his lip to endure the pain, Kwil clutched tightly at his shield. Knowing the monster would not relent peacefully, he resorted to the only plan he could think of. Drawing on the magic inside him, he placed one hand flat against the back of the shield. Adding his own heat to the stone's, he spoke a brief word of magic. The light illuminated tenfold, the shield's rays glinting off every puddle in the cave.

Roaring with displeasure, the cockatrice was forced to cease its attack and squeeze its eyes shut. Should its gaze fall upon its own reflection in one of the many pools, it would turn itself to stone. "Enough!" the beast cried. "Dim the light, and I will give you what you seek."

"How do I know I can trust you?" Kwil asked. Right now he had the upper hand, but if he doused the light, he would be at the creature's mercy.

The cockatrice lifted its foot to its beak and clamped down, severing a section of claw. Spitting it in the mage's direction, it said, "Take it and leave this place."

Kwil grabbed the claw and shuddered, imagining the damage it could have done him. It was larger than his own hand and as strong as steel. "Thank you," Kwil said. Before dimming the shield, he asked, "If it was so simple to remove the claw, and it caused you no pain, why did you make it so difficult for me?"

"Because you came uninvited to my home," the beast replied. "Normally those types become my dinner."

Kwil took that as his cue to leave. Obviously he had worn out his welcome. Keeping his reflective shield at the ready, he backed away from the monster, heading for the exit. Stepping out into the light, he broke into a run for fear the monster might pursue.

Chapter 11

"Magnificent!" Rili exclaimed, holding the claw up to the light. "Simply magnificent." Strands of blue magic pulsated through the claw as the master wizard tested its purity. Kwil had retrieved the finest specimen he'd ever seen. It would serve many purposes in the wizard's experiments.

"But how did you manage it?" Nera asked, thankful to see her friend alive.

"It was the rock formation," Kwil replied. "I was drawn to it."

"As I knew you would be," Rili said with a smirk. "Come, there is much to learn."

Satisfied that Rili hadn't intended for Kwil to be killed, Nera followed the two of them as they headed for the library. Stacks upon stacks of bookshelves lined the walls and filled the room, leaving barely enough space to squeeze between them and find what one was looking for. Rili quickly climbed a ladder and searched out several volumes, which he dropped for Kwil to catch. Only when the young man's arms were well laden did Rili cease and climb down.

"This will get you started," he said, grabbing one last book. Heading for the attached study area, he paused and asked, "You can read the runes, right?"

"Yes, Master," Kwil replied.

"Good," Rili said. "It will save us some time."

Eager to begin his lessons, Kwil took a seat and laid the books on the table before him. Rubbing his hand over their covers, he inhaled deeply, basking in the scent of the aging pages. Euphoric, he realized that this was the true beginning of his studies as a wizard. With proper training, he felt sure that one day he would become a master of the arcane. Opening his eyes, he looked upon his master. "I can't thank you enough for this opportunity," he said. "This means everything to me."

Standing above his student, Rili crossed his arms. "You speak eloquently for a slave," he said with a frown.

"My former mistress insisted on it," Kwil replied. "She's the one who taught me to read."

Still frowning, Rili replied, "That will serve you well in life, but while you're here you must pose as a slave. At least when someone comes to visit." Though Rili would have preferred to send Kwil away to a land inhabited by humans, he knew the boy might have difficulties finding a teacher. After all, he was of low birth—the same as Rili himself. "The punishment for training you would be severe," he added. "I'm sure you realize this."

Kwil nodded.

"What of your servants?" Nera asked, concerned that one of them might be willing to turn Kwil in.

With a dismissive wave of his hand, Rili said, "My two servants are sympathetic to the cause. I have entrusted them with my life, and you can as well."

Nera was satisfied with Rili's answer. The rumors she had heard about him were true. Master Rili was one of the few Gatans out there willing to help slaves escape to freedom. He was likely the only person in a thousand miles who would be willing to help Kwil learn magic. She smiled to herself, her heart full of hope for her friend. He had earned his place as an apprentice, and now he would live his dream.

As Kwil and Rili settled in for what appeared to be a long lesson, Nera decided to make herself useful. Since she'd be taking advantage of Rili's generosity, the least she could do was tend to a few chores around the house. With no talent for laundry or gardening, she decided she could help most by running errands in the nearby town. Though its citizens had proved themselves cruel and heartless in their treatment of Kwil, Nera would have to deal with them. It was the closest town to obtain supplies, the next being more than fifty miles away.

"Can I fetch you anything from town?" she asked, not bothering to wait for a break in their conversation. She knew they would likely be discussing magic until sunset, and it would be too late for her to travel.

"Yes, yes," Rili said, annoyed by the interruption. From the pocket of his robe, he produced a small bit of parchment. "These are the things I'll be needing." He handed the list to Nera without looking at her.

Nera's eyes scanned the list. She recognized most of the items and assumed the town's apothecary would know the rest. "Do you have a horse I could borrow?"

"Only one of them takes a saddle," he replied. "The black one." He flipped through the pages of an old tome, anxiously pointing to a passage he wished to share with his student.

Silently exiting the room, Nera felt a sense of relief. She had no desire to sit around all day listening to them discuss magic. Instead, she would spend an hour or two in town before returning home to work on her music. She would surprise Kwil with a song of his triumph against the cockatrice. Humming to herself, she strolled toward the stable.

Nera smiled at the sight of the black horse, its mouth shoved full of alfalfa. "Snack time's over," she said, rubbing her hand along the horse's neck. Reaching for the saddle that hung on a nearby post, she positioned it onto the horse's back. Luckily, Master Rili was not a large man. His stallion was a perfect size for Nera to ride.

Climbing into the saddle, she nudged the horse forward. His gait was smooth and easy, giving Nera the opportunity to enjoy the countryside rather than hanging on for her life. She didn't have a lot of experience with horses, her father having declared it unladylike, but she had a love of all creatures and found horses to be quite beautiful. They served her kind in return for food and affection. From what she'd seen, most horses were treated far better than human slaves.

Banishing the negativity from her mind, Nera pressed forward. If she couldn't let go of her resentment of the townspeople, she would have trouble dealing with them on Rili's behalf. She didn't have to like them, but she had to be civil, even though she would have preferred to take revenge on those who had wronged her friend. But Kwil would not want that, and Nera was trying her best to put her own feelings aside.

Thanks to the quick stride of the stallion, Nera arrived in the town much faster than she expected. Apparently she and Kwil had been more lost than she realized when looking for Rili's home. The path was easy to follow, and it was less than an hour's journey by horse.

Stopping first outside the bookseller, she tethered the horse near a trough. With a whinny, he bid her not to take too long, which brought a smile to the girl's face. Stepping inside she was nearly overwhelmed by the scent of books. Unlike her friend, she did not enjoy the smell. To her it was the odor of dust and mold.

The elderly Gatan behind the counter peered at her over his spectacles. "Yes?" he asked.

"I'm here to retrieve Master Rili's special order," Nera said.

"Ah," the man replied, rising from his seat. He fiddled for several moments with something beneath the counter before producing a bundle of books. "Here they are," he said.

"Thank you," she replied, taking the bundle. It was heavier than it looked. Returning outside, she tied the bundle to the horse, which snorted. "I don't know either," she said to the horse. "What could he possibly need with more books?" Laughing, she looked around to see if anyone had noticed her speaking to the animal. One woman was staring at her from across the path, but Nera didn't mind. She flashed a smile and continued about her business, while the woman shook her head.

Entering the apothecary's shop, she was immediately taken in by his selection of lute strings. At home she had been lucky to find three varieties. This shop carried seven—each with their own unique set of musical properties. She wondered how the strings would feel under her fingers and which would produce the purest tones. Choosing strings was a personal matter, and many well-known lute players would travel long distances to find their perfect match.

"Do you play?" a voice asked.

Jumping at the sound of his voice, Nera pressed her hand to her heart.

"I didn't mean to startle you, Miss," the man said, smiling. He was a tall Gatan with a brown pelt and long white whiskers.

"Yes, I do play," Nera replied. "You have quite a selection of strings here. I wasn't expecting that."

The man laughed. "I wanted to be a luthier when I was young, but alas I had no talent for woodwork." Opening the case, he added, "Thankfully, I'm quite good at fashioning the strings." Retrieving a set of strings, he stretched out one and extended it toward Nera. "Feel," he said.

Nera pressed the string between her fingers. It was soft but strong, and she could already hear it singing to her. Her eyes sparkling with wonder, she said, "I'd love to try them."

"These strings will take your music to new heights," the apothecary promised. Disappearing into a back room, the Gatan soon returned with a lute. "Mind you, these will sound different on your particular instrument," he said.

With a smile, Nera took the lute from him and began to play. Her fingers flew over the strings as she strummed a cheerful melody. Pausing a moment, she said, "These are wonderful!" They felt like velvet beneath her fingertips, and her heart yearned to try them on her own lute. "How much do they cost?" she dared to ask. Though she had some money, she wasn't sure how she would obtain more. She had planned only for emergencies, not luxury items.

"For a pretty girl like you?" the man replied. "Five silver." He grinned, his white teeth glistening.

Nera bit her bottom lip as she tried to rationalize the expensive purchase. The strings she was currently using were in fine condition, and there was no need to change them. But they were student quality, not at all like the ones the apothecary crafted. Knowing she would probably regret spending so much, she nodded. "I'll take them."

"Splendid," the man replied.

"Oh, and these items on Master Rili's account," she said, producing the list form her pocket.

The apothecary took the list and busied himself preparing Rili's order. Meanwhile, Nera continued to strum at the lute, her heart swelling with musical joy. She wasn't sure how much time had passed when the man finally handed her a box full of pouches and bottles. Wrapping the strings in brown paper, he placed them on top of the box.

"You're all set," he said.

Fishing out five silver pieces, she handed them to the apothecary. "Thank you," she said.

"Enjoy the strings," he replied as she stepped out the door.

Eager to return to the manor and restring her lute, Nera rushed to the stallion and secured the box behind her saddle. The horse licked her hand as she untethered him and prepared to climb aboard. A flash of green and yellow caught her eye, and she halted in her motion to see a familiar sight. The Orva family colors and crest stood out among the townspeople, and she froze on the spot. What could her father's men be doing here? Luckily they had not seen her, and she felt a strong urge to flee. Hopping into the saddle, she nudged the horse forward, prompting him to a run.

Once she could no longer see the town behind her, she slowed the horse to a walk, giving herself time to think. *Father must have business in this town,* she thought. But all his business ventures of which she was aware were far to the south, not here. Her hands trembled slightly as she gripped the reins, wondering if he might have sent his guards looking for her.

Arriving at the manor, she stabled the horse and removed its saddle. Kwil and Rili were still chatting away in the study, so she set the items she'd retrieved on a table and silently walked away. There was no need to worry them until she was certain there was trouble. For now, she decided to take her mind off the situation by restringing her lute.

Though the strings held magic for her, she still found her mind wandering as she tightened them onto her instrument. What would her father do if he found her? The thought sent a shiver through her body. Her hasty departure from the College would bring shame on their house, and Lord Orva cared more for his pride than his child. He would probably be angrier than she'd ever seen him.

Strumming at the strings, she closed her eyes and immersed herself in the melody. In music there was peace, and her cares dropped away, allowing the melody to take control of her thoughts. The new strings gave her lute a softer tone, and her fingers moved over the strings with ease. She played on till sunset, never stopping for more than a minute.

A heavy knock at the door dragged her back to reality. Her heart pounding, she knew who must be calling. Setting her lute aside, she slowly rose to her feet and crept toward the rear of the manor. Rili crossed her as he headed for the front door, but he took no notice of her behavior.

"Open up!" a gruff male voice demanded.

"Yes, yes," Rili said, his hand reaching for the latch. As he opened the door, he stared into the face of a large Gatan wearing a yellow and green tunic. "What can I do for you?" he asked, annoyed by the interruption.

"I have reason to believe Lady Nera is staying here," the man said. "Some merchants in town had dealings with her today."

Nera heard these words from the back room and knew she had erred in entering the town. Of course her father would send guards, and the townspeople would be well aware that she was new to the area. She had put herself, Kwil, and Rili in grave danger. She should have left once Kwil was accepted as Rili's student. Without a thought to her own safety, she opened the rear door and ran toward the forest.

"I've no idea who you're talking about," Rili said to the man.

"Don't make this more diff—" he started to say.

"She's running out the back!" a second guard called, cutting him off.

The guards ran for their horses, determined to cut Nera off before she could find a hiding place.

Kwil approached Master Rili from behind. "What's happened?" he asked.

"It seems Nera's family has sent some people to fetch her," Rili replied.

Kwil couldn't believe his ears. "You're not bothered by that?"

"She isn't my concern," Rili replied. "She's a noble lady, and her family won't stand for her hiding in the woods."

His casual manner infuriated Kwil. "We can't let them take her!" he shouted, immediately stepping toward the door.

Rili grabbed Kwil's arm and held tightly. "Listen," he said. "You're a slave. My slave as far as they know. If they think you had anything to do with her running away, they will drag you back with her, and her father will execute you. Don't be an idiot."

Master Rili's argument was convincing. Kwil knew interfering could mean his death. But Nera needed him. If their situations were reversed, he knew she would risk everything to help him.

Seeing that Kwil was still uneasy, Rili added, "Her parents won't hurt her. They want her home, and that's the end of it. Don't worry."

The guards easily caught up with Nera, who punched the first guard the moment he dismounted. His nose dripping with blood, he grabbed her arms and held them tightly. "We'll have no more of that!" he shouted. Though he was angry, he knew better than to harm the girl. A single scratch on her would result in severe punishment from Lord Orva.

The second guard arrived a moment later and hopped down from his horse. Using two straps of leather, he bound Nera's hands and feet, preventing her from running away. Together the two men lifted her onto the saddle, seating her sideways.

"Let me go!" Nera screamed, struggling to free her hands.

"Be still!" the guard demanded. "And no screaming or we'll gag you."

Nera narrowed her eyes at the man but said nothing. They rode past Rili's cottage, and she caught a glimpse of Kwil being dragged back inside by Rili, who was no doubt using magic to increase his strength. Wishing she had the power to speak to him without words, she thought, *I'll be all right, Kwil. Take care of yourself, and become the master wizard you've always wanted to be.* She fought back her tears, not wanting her captors to see her break down. If her father had his way, she would never see Kwil again. He would likely marry her off and send her away, where she would live out her days as a prisoner in her own home.

Chapter 12

Despite Master Rili's reassurances that Nera would be fine, Kwil could not stop worrying about her. He slept little that night, and tried to focus on his reading the next day, but his mind wandered back to his friend and her well-being. He had to do something. Who knows what her father had in store for her? Kwil knew him to be a cruel man, and his anger toward his daughter could be severe. Nera did not want to return to her parents' home, and that was all the reason Kwil needed to act.

As the sun finally began to set, Kwil made up his mind to rescue her. Rili had finished his dinner and was now soaking in his tub, giving Kwil the opportunity to move about the grounds unseen. Fastening his cloak around his shoulders, he crept out into the night. Though he wasn't a good rider, he knew he would need to borrow his master's horse. Otherwise, he was in for a long walk, and Nera might already be sent away by the time he reached the Orva manor. If he didn't act now, he might never find her.

Approaching the horse with caution, Kwil did his best to stay calm. He had worked with horses, but they intimidated him with their size and strength. If the stallion sensed his anxiety, it would put the animal on edge. Taking deep breaths, Kwil reached for the saddle and placed it on the horse's back. "Easy, boy," he said as he fastened the buckles.

Satisfied with the saddle, Kwil tried to pull himself onto the horse. His foot missed the stirrup, and he fell to the ground, landing on his backside. The horse snorted and looked away. Brushing the straw from his cloak, Kwil said, "Don't laugh." Shaking his head, he tried again, this time successfully landing in the saddle. With a gentle nudge, he urged the horse forward, but it stood its ground. Grabbing a mouthful of alfalfa, it chewed lazily, unconcerned for the young man's plight.

"We have to go," he said. "Nera needs us."

The horse was unconvinced. Kwil tried digging his heels harder, but the stallion would not budge.

Obviously his horsemanship skills left a lot to be desired. He had spent time as a groom, but he had never been a trainer or a rider. The only option left to him was magic. Searching his mind for the correct spell, he laid a hand on the horse's neck. Whispering a few words, he released white magic from his fingers, the light traveling over the stallion's body. With a whinny of agreement, the horse reared on its hind legs, forcing Kwil to hold on tightly. The steed burst forward, racing into the darkness, its eyes lit with magical light.

They raced beneath the moonlight, the young sorcerer giving only mental directions to the horse. Amazed at the effectiveness of the spell, Kwil's heart pounded with exhilaration. Their two minds had connected, allowing the horse a clear view of its destination, while Kwil felt the surge of adrenaline brought on by the horse's exertions. Never before had he experienced such freedom. The stallion loved to run, and it shared the young man's determination to rescue his friend. Working as one, the two galloped through the night, racing on till dawn.

* * * * *

Dragging Nera by her arms, the guards brought her before her father. Struggling all the way, Nera tried to break free of her captors. They tightened their grip, angering the girl further. The blood rising to her face, she bared her fangs at the men.

Lord Orva waved his hand. "Release her," he commanded them.

The guards immediately let go of her, and she snatched her arms away from them. Turning to one of the guards, Nera spit in his face. He clenched his jaw in anger, but said nothing. A severe look from Lord Orva reminded him of his duty to the family. He backed away without harming the girl while the second guard loosened her bonds.

"Leave us," Orva demanded. Staring into his daughter's eyes, he said, "How could you bring such shame on our family?"

Swallowing hard, Nera replied, "You're the shameful one! You call it honor, but it's your pride that matters. You care more for your pride than your child."

"What would you know of honor?" he asked, shaking his head. "Disappearing with a slave?"

"I'm of age," she reminded him. "I can do whatever I want."

"You most certainly cannot," he replied. "You will obey me until the day I die!" He raised a hand to strike her, but she did not flinch. Lowering his hand, he said, "Your teacher visited me and told me what happened. It cost me a great deal to buy her silence."

"I don't care who knows I helped a slave," Nera replied, her chin held high. "I'd do it again if I had to."

"To save face, your teacher has put out the rumor that you left school for health reasons," he said, ignoring his daughter's words. "So we have a bit of time while I search for an appropriate husband for you."

Her eyes wide, Nera looked over at her mother, who was now visibly pregnant. "Are you going to let him sell me off?" she asked.

"You're not cattle, my dear," her mother replied. "If you won't be attending the College, it's time you were married." Stroking her husband's arm, she said, "Perhaps the baby will be the wizard you've always wanted in the family."

Nera grunted in frustration. How could her mother condone this? "I'm a free woman!" she shouted. "I'm not some slave you can sell into marriage!" Fuming with anger, she tried to walk away, but Orva grabbed her arm, holding her in place.

"Let go of me!" she demanded.

Without releasing his grip, he said, "You will do as you're told and marry whomever I desire. You have a duty to this family, and you will not bring shame on us again."

"If I marry, my duty will be to my husband," she reminded him. "I'll do everything I can to expose you as a liar and a swindler." She was not ignorant to his business dealings, and she knew he was involved in questionable practices. It wouldn't take much to ruin his name should such accusations be brought about by his own daughter.

"Your husband is irrelevant!" he shouted. "I will own him as I do you. Don't expect you'll be living a life of luxury after this stunt."

Nera narrowed her eyes but said nothing. She knew exactly what he meant. He would sell her in marriage to a lesser noble, one he could control. The pair would live at the mercy of her father, dependent on him for all their funds.

"Guards!" Orva called. "Take her to her room and make sure she remains there."

166

The guards grabbed her arms and forced her to walk forward. "I'm not your slave!" she cried. "You can't do this to me!"

"You are a disgrace to this family," he replied. "When you're ready to cooperate, you will be released."

Fighting all the way up the stairs, she called back, "Then I guess I'll be locked up forever!"

Shoving her inside her room, the guards closed her door and took positions outside. Nera cried out in anger, not knowing what to do next. She would not marry anyone at her father's insistence, that much was certain. No matter how far she had to run, or how many times he dragged her back, she would resist him. She would not be broken.

Pacing across the room, she swished her tail and tried to think of a way to escape. Eventually they'd have to open the door to feed her. Perhaps she could make a run for it then. Sitting near the window with a huff, she stared out at the stars. Tears formed in her eyes, and she felt embarrassed at the weakness. *No, tears are not a weakness,* she told herself.

As she stared into the darkness, her thoughts turned to Kwil. How readily he had accepted his role as a slave. To be completely under the control of another person was unfathomable, but here Nera was in the same situation. Her father was determined to keep her in his grasp despite her being of age. Maybe if she seemed cooperative, she would have an easier time getting away. If her father trusted her again, he wouldn't watch her every move.

The thought of playing along made her ill, but it was worth a try. It might be her best chance for escape. Maybe then she could find her way back to Rili's manor, if for no other reason than to say goodbye to Kwil. She didn't want to put him in danger, but she couldn't stand the thought of never seeing him again. Once she was settled elsewhere, the two could keep in touch through letters.

A smile appeared on her face as she finalized her plans. Life would not be so dismal after all. She would find work as a musician and travel the land, never revealing her family name. The freedom she craved would be hers.

* * * * *

Arriving at the outskirts of the Orva property, Kwil climbed down from the saddle. He was stiff and sore from his long ride, but glad to have finally arrived.

Patting the horse's side, he said, "I need you to stay here and wait for me."

The stallion grunted in response.

"I'll take that to mean you're in agreement," Kwil said. Their minds remained locked as long as they were in physical contact, but now that Kwil had to move away from the horse, he wasn't sure if the magic would last. He could only hope the horse would still be waiting for him once he returned with Nera.

Tiptoeing across the manor grounds, Kwil was thankful for the cover of darkness. Clouds had rolled in, concealing him from the moonlight, and there appeared to be no one patrolling the grounds. Getting inside the manor was necessary but risky. Anyone he encountered might raise the alarm. He could think of only one person besides Nera who could be trusted not to betray him.

Approaching the door to the kitchens, he strained his eyes to see in the darkness. Pausing a moment, he listened for footsteps or any other sound that might betray the approach of a guard. He heard nothing. Remembering to breathe, he pulled the handle and opened the door only an inch. Inside a fire burned brightly, a sure sign that someone was awake. *Please let it be Jenn*, he thought.

Opening the door a bit wider, he peered inside. The figure of an elderly woman sat churning butter for the morning's breakfast. With a sigh of relief, Kwil stepped inside. "Jenn," he whispered, stepping cautiously toward the old woman. He had no desire to startle her. If she cried out, he would certainly be caught.

The old woman showed no signs of hearing him, so he tried again, this time louder. "Jenn," he said. "It's me, Kwil."

The old woman turned around and clamped a hand over her mouth. Rising to her feet, she threw her arms around the young man's neck and squeezed as tight as she could. "By all the stars," she said. "It's really you." Tears glistened in her eyes as she looked him over. "And you're the picture of health too," she added.

"It's good to see you," he replied. The look of pride on the old woman's face gave him pause. She had been so kind to him, and he didn't realize how much he missed her until this moment.

"Did you find your freedom?" she asked.

"I did," he replied. "I'm going to be a master sorcerer someday."

Slapping him on the shoulder, the old woman asked, "Then why'd you come back here? It's not safe!"

"I had to," he said. "Nera's in trouble."

"You will be too if you're caught," she said. Shaking her head, she added, "Imagine a slave going free and then coming back here."

"Do you know where Nera is?" he asked, ignoring her comment. "I have to find her."

"They've locked her in her room," Jenn replied. "I heard Lord Orva say he plans to marry her off."

"Have they mistreated her?" he wondered.

Jenn shook her head. "As far as I know she's been treated well, but there are guards posted at her door. Don't you dare think of going up there."

"I have to find a way," Kwil said. He turned to exit but only took one step before looking back. "Come with us," he said. "You don't have to remain a slave."

"Hush," the old woman replied, waving her hand. "Whether I'm cooking here or somewhere else doesn't matter. These old bones of mine are fine right here."

Kwil's heart sank, but he understood. Hugging her goodbye, he said, "Be well. I'll miss you."

"Go on now and be a wizard," she said, giving him a push. She watched as he walked away, a twinkle of pride in her eyes.

Stepping out into the darkness, Kwil made his way to the side of the manor. Looking up, he could see light in Nera's open window. Relieved that she was still awake, he searched for a way to climb up the wall. There was no rope or ladder nearby, and he knew no spell that could make him jump thirty feet off the ground.

Searching his mind, he tried to think of a spell that might work. Remembering an incantation that would produce a sticky resin on the caster's hands, he had to contain his laughter. When he'd read about it, he couldn't imagine what possible use this spell would have. Now he knew. If his hands were sticky enough, he could climb the wall without the aid of a rope.

Repeating the incantation four times, the spell finally succeeded. A small amount of amber resin oozed from his pores, and he placed a hand against the wood. His hand stuck, but not enough to pull his weight. Again he spoke the words to produce more resin, but nothing happened. Closing his eyes, he took a few deep breaths to clear his mind. This had to work.

His only other choice was to go back inside and risk running into the guards.

Reaching deep into his magical stores, he pulled at the energy inside. Focusing his mind to the words, he whispered them to the night. With his full intentions focused on the spell, a soft green glow spread over his hands. The resin dripped from his fingers, and his feet felt sticky in his boots. Kicking them off, he placed both hands and feet against the wooden wall. Pulling himself up, he climbed without looking down. His sight focused on Nera's window, he climbed until he could see inside.

Hearing scratching against her windowsill, Nera grabbed a nearby vase and crept toward the window. Raising the vase to strike the intruder, she nearly brought it down on Kwil's head. Recognizing her friend, she immediately set her weapon aside. "Kwil," she whispered. "Is it really you?"

Grinning, he nodded his head. "It's me."

Nera couldn't contain her excitement. She leaned toward the window and kissed his forehead. "I'm so glad to see you," she said. Now she would not have to play along with her father's plans. "How did you get up here?"

Raising a hand to show her the resin, he said, "Sticky hands."

Nodding slowly, she asked, "How am I going to get down?"

Kwil wasn't sure. The spell probably wasn't strong enough to carry the two of them.

"Hold on," Nera said, moving away from the window. Grabbing a tapestry of her family crest from the wall, she tossed it to the floor. Taking the rope attached to it, she returned to the window and presented it to Kwil.

"That's only two feet long," he said. "That's not going to get you to the ground."

Rolling her eyes, Nera replied, "Use magic on it."

Slightly embarrassed, Kwil took the rope in one sticky hand. Focusing his mind to the rope, he spread a soft white light over its surface. The rope began to grow, twisting itself as it stretched toward the ground. Once it was long enough, he handed it back to Nera.

Tying the rope to her bedpost, Nera said, "All set." Sitting on the windowsill, she grasped the rope in both hands before swinging her feet outside. Surprising even herself, Nera proved a nimble rope climber. Kwil moved slowly at her side, prepared to catch her should she fall, but she did not need his help. Her feet reached the ground in safety.

"Let's get out of here," she said.

Shoving his feet back inside his boots, Kwil agreed. "The horse is this way," he said, leading her away from the manor.

To their delight, the horse was waiting for them only steps from where Kwil had left him. He neighed softly at the sight of Nera. Climbing aboard the saddle, they galloped away toward freedom.

Chapter 13

After riding through the night, Kwil and Nera found themselves near the College grounds by morning. There was little activity, most of the students having not yet risen from their beds. Kwil wondered what the day's lessons would be, but it mattered not. In a few hours, they would be back at Rili's house, where he could continue to learn.

"We don't want to linger here," Nera cautioned. "My father may have paid off Mistress Tress, but that doesn't mean she'll actually keep her mouth shut. There could be people looking for you." After a pause, she added, "Looking for both of us."

Nodding his understanding, Kwil spurred the horse forward. The path was dry, providing them with easy passage. Many other travelers crossed their path, but none paid them any heed. Kwil was grateful for that. Word of Nera's escape had not yet spread through the area, and he hoped they could make it safely to Rili's before it did.

By evening, the two arrived at the manor house, and Rili stepped out to meet them. With his arms crossed against his chest, he scowled at the pair. "At least you've returned my horse," he said, scolding.

Climbing down from the saddle, Kwil said, "Forgive me, Master. I could not leave Nera to an uncertain fate."

Nera said nothing. She knew Rili would ask her to leave, and she was prepared for it. Her presence would bring trouble and prevent Kwil from learning. She had to leave.

Sighing, Rili said, "I'm sorry, Kwil. I won't be able to teach you."

Kwil stammered as he started to speak. "Because I disobeyed you?" he asked. "This was a special situation. Believe me, it won't happen again."

Shaking his head, the master wizard replied, "It makes no difference. Her family won't stop looking for her, and this is where they will look first. I can't risk having trouble like that around here. It would jeopardize everything." With guards poking around, he would likely be discovered as a proponent of abolishing slavery. His operation would be brought to a halt, and escaped slaves would have to travel weeks in the wilderness to find help.

"Please," Nera begged. "I will go away and never return, but you have to teach Kwil."

"The guards will undoubtedly return," Rili stated. "One of them might recognize Kwil, and I'll have no way to protect him." His voice was full of regret. He truly wished he could help young Kwil, but it was impossible.

"It's all right," Kwil replied. Turning to Nera, he added, "I wouldn't want to stay if you left. I'd be worried about you."

"I can take care of myself," she said. "I'll join a troupe somewhere, and then I can write to you. You have to learn. Please, Master Rili, teach him."

"I'm finished repeating myself," Rili replied. "Take your lute and leave this place. I'm sorry, Kwil. I will not mention to anyone that you passed this way again."

"Where will we go?" Kwil asked.

"If you still want to learn magic, you might find help in the Dark Forest," Rili said. "Mistress Seela lives in a cottage a few days' journey from here. She took me as her apprentice when no one else would. She taught me many things, and there is much yet I did not learn. If you truly wish to learn great things, learn from her."

"How will I know her?" Kwil asked, suddenly eager to get going.

"I doubt you will encounter many Gatans in those woods, and none like Seela," Rili replied. "She is a Feles."

Nera gasped in surprise. She had seen one Feles before as a child, and the sight had stuck with her.

"What's a Feles?" Kwil asked. The term was entirely foreign to him.

"A Feles is a Gatan of special birth," Nera explained. "They are small and walk on four legs. It's said they are the manifestation of our ancestors." Wrinkling her brow, she said, "They are usually revered, and people pay a lot of money to see them. I can't imagine one living in obscurity in the Dark Forest."

"That is all I'm prepared to say," Rili said. "You may seek her out and tell her that I sent you. Otherwise, you may go where you will." Grabbing the horse's lead, he walked away toward the stable.

"Dark Forest it is then," Kwil said.

Nodding, Nera said, "Looks like it. Let's get our things."

The two entered the manor one last time to collect their few belongings. Caressing her lute case, Nera realized how much she had missed holding it. Never again would they part—not for her father, nor any other villain who would try to destroy her spirit.

As they exited the house and headed toward the woods, they saw no sign of Rili. Kwil wanted to say goodbye, but Nera stopped him. "I'm sure he feels bad about this," she said. "He does want to help you, but he also wants to help other slaves. With my father's men keeping watch over him, he wouldn't be able to do either."

"I couldn't turn my back on you, Nera," Kwil said. "Even if it means I can't learn magic."

Kwil's loyalty made Nera feel small. Was she worthy of such dedication? "Kwil, I would see you live your dream," she said. "I wouldn't expect you to follow me while I pursue mine. The time may come when we are forced to part."

Kwil stared down at his feet. "I couldn't leave you to suffer at your father's hands," he said. "You would have come for me. But if you want me to go on without you, I'll respect that."

"We'll find Seela together," Nera replied. "After you're settled, I might have to leave. I don't think she can teach me music." She managed a weak smile, hoping her friend understood. "It wouldn't be the end of our friendship, you know. You can come see me play, and I can marvel at your great feats of magic."

Kwil laughed. "It's a deal," he said, throwing an arm over her shoulder. They'd come through too much not to remain friends, even if their separate paths meant they couldn't always be together. For now, he would enjoy her company and not dwell on what was to come.

A servant stepped out of the manor and approached the travelers at the tree line. "Master Rili asked me to bring you some food for your journey." Extending two bundles toward the pair, she nodded before turning away.

"Thank him for us," Nera called after her. Peeking inside the bundle she saw fresh bread, dried fruit and strips of meat. "It's better than eating pinecones," she said with a smirk.

"That's probably all we'll find on our own," Kwil replied, taking a pinch of bread. Having snuck out the previous night without dinner, he was already famished.

"I wonder why he wouldn't give more details about Mistress Seela," Nera said.

Shrugging, Kwil replied, "Maybe she practices dark magic. That would certainly make her an outcast."

Her eyes wide, Nera asked, "Would you want to study with someone like that?"

"I don't have to learn anything evil," he replied. "If she can teach me what I need to know, then I'm willing to learn. Besides, just because someone knows dark magic doesn't make them evil."

"What does it make them?" she asked.

"Well read?" he replied, a little uncertain. "It doesn't matter," he added. "No one else is going to teach me. We don't know why she lives as an outcast, but I imagine we'll find out." Slinging his pack over his shoulder, he marched through the trees.

"Wait!" Nera called after him.

He paused to look at her. "What is it?"

"Do you know which way to go? Have you been to the Dark Forest before?"

"Not exactly," he replied. "But my former mistress used to love scary stories that took place there. Didn't you ever read those as a kit?"

"I was never allowed to read anything interesting," she responded.

"Well, I saw a map in one of her books. It lies southeast of here."

"And you think that's reliable?" she asked, crossing her arms. "Maybe we should go back and get better directions."

"The Dark Forest is a place of magic," Kwil replied. "I can sense its pull as we get closer. Trust me." He gave a crooked smile and cocked his head to the side.

Sighing, she said, "All right. Just don't take us near that cockatrice."

"It's that way," he said, pointing the opposite direction. "I don't think it'll bother us."

Wrapping their cloaks tightly around them, they tried to block out the cold. It was a windy day, and the exertion of walking still wasn't enough to keep them warm. After an hour, Nera could bear the silence no longer.

"This is turning into a long, cold trip," she said. "I can't play my lute and walk, so you'll have to entertain me."

"You want to see some magic?" he asked.

"Only if it involves getting warm," she replied. "Talk to me. Tell me a story or something. Maybe one about the Dark Forest."

Kwil thought for a moment. "There are ogres living there, you know."

"I don't want to hear that story," Nera replied. "Are there any nice stories about where we're going?"

"There's one about a little girl and a bear," he said. "But the bear eats her at the end, so I guess that isn't exactly nice."

"No, it isn't," Nera said. "Tell me about your father. You said you've dreamed of your mother, but you didn't mention him. Do you ever see him?"

"I don't," he admitted. "To be honest, I'm not sure if he ever saw me. I don't think slave breeders care to keep families together for long."

Frowning, she replied, "You're right about that. I've seen toddlers auctioned off." Even as a child, Nera felt slavery was wrong. With her own eyes she'd seen humans inspected like cattle and sold to the highest bidder. Children were ripped away from their parents, and husbands were taken from their wives. How could her people justify such behavior? Her father had told her that humans do not feel love the same way Gatans do. But that wasn't true. To look into their eyes as they were separated from their families was all the proof she needed. And then there was Kwil. He was completely devoted to her, even

185

though he was no longer her servant. If only all Gatans could see humans the way she did. Her heart heavy, she said, "I guess that didn't turn out to be such a nice subject either."

Kwil paused in his walking and turned to face her. "Maybe my father was some magical creature," he said, attempting to lighten the mood. He seriously doubted it was the case, but it was worth a shot to cheer his friend. "Maybe he was a unicorn."

Nera laughed. "Maybe he was," she replied, grinning.

Walking again, Kwil said, "You could have magical parents too, you know. Maybe you were adopted."

Still smiling, she replied, "They stole me right out of my crib. My dragon mother was devastated." Laughing, she added, "Maybe Mistress Seela can teach me how to breathe fire."

They both laughed and continued joking back and forth until the sun had nearly disappeared from the sky. Choosing a suitable place to spend the night, they dropped their bags and settled in.

Kwil prepared a fire and fed the flames with magic to increase the heat. "That should keep us warm till morning," he announced.

"Will it keep predators away?" Nera wondered. There were bears in this area, and the cockatrice wasn't far enough away for her liking.

"I can take care of that," he said proudly. Walking in a circle, he placed a ring of magic around their campsite. "This will protect us," he said. "No one can enter this space without my permission."

"Unless it's a wizard," she pointed out. Someone with greater magical knowledge could easily break his spell. She hadn't had much interest in her studies at the College, but she'd seen enough duels to know that wizards often tried to best one another.

"I don't suspect a lot of wizards will be walking around here tonight," he said dismissively. "Most of them have nice homes to go to. Bandits might be more likely."

"You're probably right about the wizards," she replied. "Bandits usually stay closer to the road. It's easier to rob merchants that way." Scooting close to the fire, Nera took out her lute. "Do you mind if I play a while?" she asked.

"I'd enjoy it," he replied.

She plucked softly at the strings and hummed along with it. When she finished, she strained her ears to the night. "It's so quiet," she commented. "No owls, no wolves, nothing." The silence was unnerving, so she played another song to ease her mind.

Kwil lay back on the ground and stared up at the stars, falling asleep to the sound of Nera's lute. His dreams filled with visions of music, and all the colors that accompanied it. A vision of his mother also appeared, her soft voice singing along with the strumming of the lute.

Nera played late into the night before finally drifting off to sleep, her lute still clutched in her hands. Images of travel came to her mind, the cold wind blowing as she walked. Fear and panic overcame her as she realized she was alone. Kwil was nowhere to be found. She called for him, but he did not respond. The snow grew deep beneath her feet, and the gusting wind blinded her. She was lost in the Dark Forest with no one to help her find her way.

Sinking to her knees in the snow, she wondered where Kwil had gone. Had he been hurt or had he simply abandoned her? How would she survive? Looking up to the sky, she saw the silhouette of a dragon, its massive wings fanned wide. It was her mother come to fetch her and return her to the nest. Standing, she held her arms wide, ready to embrace the dragon as it descended toward her. As the creature alighted beside her, she awoke, finding herself still in the forest, Kwil snoring softly near the fire.

Sitting up, she stared into the fire and tried to recall all the images of her dream. It was silly to imagine a dragon as a parent, but it was far better than reality. Dragons were free, as she was now. Smiling to herself, she realized how much she and Kwil truly had in common. Reclining once more, she settled in for the night, welcoming the dream dragon's return.

Chapter 14

The following day was bitterly cold, but otherwise uneventful. The two trudged on, attempting to keep their spirits high despite the freezing weather. Kwil worked on a spell to keep his body warm, but he failed in his attempt to share it with Nera. Attempts to teach her the spell ended in failure as well. Either she didn't have the skill, or she didn't have the drive. Kwil gave her an extra portion of his own food to help her keep warm as they walked.

By the middle of the third day, the forest began to change. No longer were the trees a familiar silver. Instead, they were deep brown, some of them black in color. Dark red and purple leaves littered the forest floor, and unseen creatures scurried beneath them. Long, thorn-covered vines descended from the treetops. Despite the lack of a leaf canopy, the light of the sun barely reached through the forest. The trees were densely packed, their dark coloration absorbing the majority of the light.

"I don't like the look of this place," Kwil said, taking in his surroundings.

"Is it different from the stories you read?" Nera asked.

"No, it's just how I pictured it," he replied. The entire area was dark and foreboding. With every step, he expected something to jump out and grab him, exactly as it had the characters in the stories he had read. If any of those stories were true, all manner of strange creatures lived within the borders of this forest.

"If it's what you expected, why are you so nervous?" Nera asked, making note of his rapid breathing.

"It's one thing to see it in your mind," he said, "and another to actually walk in it." A shrill cry rang out, the young man crouching in response. "That sounded close," he said, swallowing hard.

"That was miles from here," Nera said, her ears turning to face the sound. "Come on." She stepped forward, gesturing for him to follow. "I'll keep you safe," she promised, grinning.

"What manner of creature makes that sound?" he wondered aloud.

"Let's hope we don't find out," Nera responded.

Pressing deeper into the Dark Forest, Kwil sensed a change in the air. Not only was it denser, there was a strong presence of magic, and it was not friendly. "Something is nearby," he said, his voice cracking slightly.

"What?" Nera asked. "A person? A creature? A trap?" She swiveled her head in all directions, taking in her surroundings. Yes, the area looked ominous, but she felt nothing out of the ordinary.

Kwil shook his head. "I'm not sure. I think we should be on our guard." The uneasy feeling would not leave him. It might have been the stories he read about the forest, but it felt more real than any tale from a book. There was something in these woods that didn't want him there, and he could feel its eyes staring at him.

"Look!" Nera shouted, startling Kwil. She pointed to a long, thin strip of a glistening substance covering the ground. "What is that?"

Kwil knelt next to the silvery strip and said, "It looks like something left a trail." Leaning down, he could smell its putrid odor. Clamping his hand over his nose and mouth, he nearly gagged. Moving back to Nera, he said, "Whatever made that trail has to be the nastiest thing I've ever smelled."

"Let's hope we don't run into it then," she replied, urging him forward. "Do you sense anything of Mistress Seela?"

Unfortunately, he did not. He could not discern the source of the magic he felt, only its presence or absence. As far as he knew, only ancient objects put off such sensations. The feeling in this forest was much different than he'd had near the stones, and he couldn't tell whether it was really a creature watching him or his own mind inventing trouble.

Not paying attention to his feet, Kwil caught his boot against a leaf-covered root and fell hard on his knees. His hand landed in another trail of shiny slime and stuck to the ground. "It's sticky!" he yelled, disgusted. Nera gaped open-mouthed as Kwil tried to free his hand. Reaching down to add her strength to his, Nera helped him pull free.

"Thanks," he said, looking down at his hand. The putrid slime coated his palm, bringing dirt and debris with it.

"I hope you know a spell to wash that off," Nera stated. "Otherwise you'll be sticking to everything you touch."

Kwil searched his mind for a spell that might work. He hadn't bothered to learn a spell that could replace a bath, so he tried several before one finally had some effect on the slime. The remaining residue he wiped against the trunk of a tree. It was then he caught sight of the creature leaving the trails. "It's a slug," he announced, pointing to a large black mass stuck to the side of a tree.

Nera moved forward to inspect it. It had no visible eyes or parts, only a globular body that moved slowly along its way, putting off a foul odor as it went. "That's disgusting," she said, stepping backward. A shriek sounded from behind her as she collided with something unseen. Spinning around, she came face to face with a snarling monster. It stood only half her height with pale gray skin and a long pointed nose. It bared its sharp, yellowed fangs at her, hissing a warning.

Nera suppressed the urge to scream, not wanting to give the creature the satisfaction. Instead, she backed away, taking a few slow steps in Kwil's direction. The monster slashed a clawed hand at her, growling low in its throat.

"What is that thing?" she whispered.

"It looks like an imp," Kwil replied.

"Can you fight it off?" she asked.

Kwil stared into its coal-black eyes, hoping it would not attack if they remained still. "I don't know," he replied. "I think they can cast a spell or two, but I don't know much more about them." He hadn't spent much time learning about creatures of magic. Instead, he had focused his attention on memorizing spells and casting them properly. He could only hope that one of the spells he was good at would suffice to defend them if the monster attacked.

Nera flinched as the imp unfurled its leathery wings. "It's about to strike," she whispered to Kwil. "Do something."

Stepping in front of his friend, Kwil did his best to look intimidating. He straightened his back and poised his hands to defend himself with magic. His heart racing, he found it impossible to focus on a single spell. Which one would be enough to stop it? Was an imp resistant to anything? There was no time to dwell on his lack of education. The monster shifted its weight, the muscles in its thighs tightening.

As the creature leapt, Kwil blasted a stream of silver sparks, knocking it to the ground. Its body fell limp, rolling over twice. Nera and Kwil took the opportunity to run, dodging limbs and pushing vines aside as they tried to put distance between themselves and the creature. They hadn't run far before they heard its shrill cry behind them.

"I hope you have something stronger for the next shot!" Nera called to her companion. "That thing's mad now."

Kwil looked back to see how much time he had to think of another spell. The imp was gaining ground, its wings helping it glide easily between the trees. Jumping to the side, Kwil narrowly avoided a stump that was partially hidden beneath the leaves. His heart pounding in his ears, he knew he had to think of something. He couldn't keep this pace much longer.

Nera's agile legs carried her with ease over the obstacles in her path. Kwil was trailing behind, so she slowed her pace, hoping to keep stride with him. Grabbing his arm, she tried to drag him faster than his legs were able to go. "Don't you have a spell that can make you run faster?" she asked.

Kwil shook his head. Such a spell would be quite useful right now, but he had yet to study any spells that could change his physicality. The imp was drawing closer, swooping toward the pair as they continued to run. Scanning his memory for a spell that might protect them, Kwil's mind went blank. He did not know how to create a shield, nor did he know any way to make either of them less susceptible to the monster's claws. His mind distracted by his shortcomings, he found it difficult to concentrate on any one spell.

The imp swooped low, its screeching voice announcing its impending attack. Nera ducked, narrowly avoiding its razor-sharp claws. It hissed and spat as it darted to the side, readying itself for another try.

"It's coming again!" Nera called out. "Try any spell!" She didn't care what he threw at the imp, as long as he was trying. Maybe he could at least slow it down.

As it drew near, Kwil could almost feel its hot breath on his neck. The thought of heat gave Kwil an idea. His most successful spells involved heat, and he had completely neglected them. Chiding himself for not going with his strengths on the first try, he stopped dead in his tracks.

Nera paused as well, waiting to see what her friend would do. She would not continue running without him.

Reaching deep into his magical stores, Kwil focused his mind to heat. A fire burned inside him, his midsection growing uncomfortably hot. Despite the burning from within, he kept his thoughts focused and his hands steady. Squeezing his eyes shut, he projected fire at the imp. The creature tucked its wings, rolling to the side and narrowly avoiding the brunt of the flames. Only a small portion of its face had been singed.

Opening his eyes to see his failure, Kwil immediately tried again. Shouting the incantation, he forced the heat to expand, conjuring a flame in the palm of his hand. But the creature was too fast. Before Kwil could unleash his spell, the imp leapt for him, sinking its teeth into the young man's shoulder.

"Kwil!" Nera shouted, running to his aid. With a low growl, she pounced on the imp, slashing at it with her claws. It shrieked in pain, kicking wildly with its muscular legs. One struck Nera's ribs, sending her rolling to the side. She was more irritated than injured as she dug her heels into the ground and righted herself.

Scrambling to his feet, Kwil blasted energy at the imp, forcing it to its knees. Targeting the trees, Kwil loosened vines and limbs, dropping them on top of the beast. The creature keeled over with an audible crack, and Kwil was certain the imp was gravely wounded.

Nera had seen enough. "Let's go!" she shouted. The creature was down, and it was time they made their escape.

Without argument, Kwil ran alongside Nera. Only steps away, they heard the imp's shriek once again. It was pursuing on foot, its wings too badly damaged to fly. Both hung at odd angles, a broken tip of bone sticking out of the left one.

"Why doesn't it stay down?" Nera asked, frustrated.

"I didn't think it would get up that quickly," Kwil replied. "What now?"

"Keep running!" she shouted.

The two ran on, but the imp was still faster than Kwil despite its injuries. Nera kept pace, wishing her companion were more athletic. The footsteps behind her were closing in, and its sights were set on Kwil.

Unable to speed his steps, Nera shoved Kwil with all her strength, forcing him to the ground. The imp missed his target, its clawed hand slashing at the air where Kwil had been. Its other hand came down awkwardly, catching the strap attached to Nera's lute case and knocking it to the ground.

Reeling in anger, Nera dropped low, running on four limbs as her ancestors had. Leaping at the imp, she knocked it off balance, the two of them tumbling over a bed of dried leaves. Not giving the monster a chance to fight back, Nera sank her fangs into its neck. Holding the bite longer than necessary, she waited for the life to drain from the creature. Once she was satisfied it wouldn't rise again, she released it and stood upright, wiping the blood from her mouth.

Kwil stared at his friend in disbelief. Her actions reminded him of the wildcats that he'd read about in tales of other lands. "I can't believe you killed it," he said, looking at the lifeless imp. "You were amazing."

"Sometimes we have to revert to the predator methods of our forefathers," she said, still breathing heavily. "What did your forefathers do?"

"Not that," he replied. "They probably just threw things." Still staring at the imp, he asked, "Why didn't you do that in the first place? It worked better than my attempts."

Shrugging, she replied, "I guess I wasn't mad enough." After a pause, she added, "And you injured him. I don't think I could have done that if he had full strength."

"I'm not so sure," he replied. "At any rate, I'm glad to be on your good side."

Nera grabbed her lute case from the ground and slung it over her back. Before she could suggest they keep going, a raucous noise erupted from the trees. Looking up, she counted a score of imps, all waiting high in the boughs, their fangs bared. The travelers were surrounded.

Chapter 15

Spinning around, Nera looked up at the trees. The imps stared back at her, their black eyes glistening in the pale light. Screeching and pounding on their chests, the monsters descended the limbs, closing in on the travelers.

Kwil dipped his head, his hands outstretched at waist level, his palms facing the ground. Repeating the same incantation three times, his voice growing louder each time, he summoned the magic inside him. Desperately grabbing at the energy all around him, he channeled it through his hands and projected it at the ground. A shockwave of energy erupted from the sorcerer, narrowly missing Nera as it extended outward. The imps reached the ground in time to be thrown aside, their limp bodies flying in all directions.

No words were necessary as the pair took to their feet, running for their lives. The previous imp recovered far too quickly, and these likely would as well. Kwil and Nera's only chance to escape them was to get a head start and find a place to hide.

Dodging trees and slipping on dried leaves, the two moved as fast as they could. Kwil stayed two steps behind Nera, though he suspected she was deliberately moving slower to match his stride. Focusing his mind to heat, he attempted to push the warmth to his leg muscles. The spell did not have the desired effect. Instead of augmenting his strength, it felt like his legs were being twisted and ripped from his body. Groaning in agony, he tried to push through the pain.

Steps ahead, Nera pointed into the distance. "Smoke!" she shouted. "There's smoke ahead!"

Kwil spotted a single line of silver smoke rising over the trees. "It must be a campsite!" he called back.

Nera clenched her jaw, hoping the camp would be full of Gatans or humans, not more imps. As she rounded a bend, she saw a small cabin, its chimney exhaling the smoke. "It's a house!" she cried, her heart pounding in her chest. Instead of an open campsite, a sturdy stone cottage awaited their arrival. It would provide far better shelter than she had expected. With any luck, the homeowner would be willing to help.

The crunching of leaves behind them heralded the approach of the imps. The cabin was still half a mile away, and Kwil was tiring fast, thanks to his mistake with the heat spell. The bite wound in his shoulder was also throbbing, adding greatly to his discomfort. Glancing down at his pierced flesh, he was shocked to see a yellowish ring surrounding it. The monster's bite contained venom.

Feeling a sudden dizziness, Kwil stumbled, but Nera was there to steady him. Placing his arm around her neck, she helped support his weight as they ran. His feet kept moving, but his head hung loosely against Nera's shoulder, the poison leaving a faint yellow trace as it traveled up his neck.

Only feet from the door, the imps caught up to their prey. Bowling them over, they shrieked with delight before forming a tight circle around the hapless pair. Kwil lay motionless on the ground, his muscles aching and burning. His mind remained unaffected, but he could do nothing more than watch as the imps closed in.

Scrambling to her feet, Nera bared her fangs at the imps, daring them to come closer. If she was going to die here, she was going to die fighting. Hissing and salivating, the monsters lunged at one another, competing to be the first to sink their teeth into the travelers. Nera swiped her claws at them, her green eyes fierce with rage.

Kwil struggled under his paralysis, trying desperately to move. Only his eyes responded to the request, allowing him to see the fate that awaited him. Incantations came and went from his mind, but without the ability to move his lips or his hands, he failed to cast a single spell. Powerless and frozen to the ground, he could only watch as the imps moved in for the kill.

Nera crouched low, positioning herself for a fight. All around her the monsters crept closer, their black eyes fixated on her. She could see a hint of fear on some of their faces. Maybe they'd seen what she did to their friend. The thought brought a slight smile to her face. At least she had taken out one. Maybe she could kill a few more before they managed to overwhelm her.

From the corner of her eye, Nera saw the door to the cabin swing open. What appeared in the doorway nearly took her breath away. Out stepped a sleek black panther, her golden eyes gleaming in the fading light.

The imps took notice of the beast as well, shrieking in terror. Flapping their wings, they fled in all directions, narrowly avoiding a collision with the galloping panther. She ran forward on silent paws, scattering the monsters. None remained behind. Their cries grew more distant as they disappeared among the trees.

The panther swung her head around, observing the odd pair who had entered her forest. Nera straightened her back and steadied her breathing, fearing not the creature who had saved her life.

"We don't want any trouble," Nera said. "My friend is hurt."

The panther approached, narrowing her eyes. With a light growl, she sniffed at the air. "What happened to him?" she asked in a smooth alto voice.

"One of the imps bit him," Nera replied. "They would have killed us if you hadn't shown up. Thank you." She nodded her appreciation to the panther.

As the panther approached Kwil, Nera stepped in front of him to block her path.

"I can help him," the panther said.

Cringing slightly at her approach, Nera hoped the panther had good intentions. If she'd wanted them dead, she could have left them to the imps. Nera decided to trust her and stepped out of the way.

Kwil could only stare wide eyed as the large cat approached and sniffed him. Laying a massive paw on his forehead, she spread white magic throughout his body. Holding the spell for a few seconds, she released the paralysis that was plaguing the young mage.

Kwil sat up slowly, wiggling his fingers to make sure they still worked. A wave of dizziness swept over him but soon passed. Climbing to his feet was awkward at first, but he managed to steady himself.

"The pain is gone," he said, grateful to the panther.

"The poison is still in your system," she replied. "We must get you inside."

After taking two steps, the panther began to shrink. Her size decreased until she was no more than the size of the housecats that sometimes appeared in the stories Kwil had read. No one kept such pets on Gi'gata, so he couldn't be absolutely certain.

"How did you do that?" Kwil asked, already knowing the answer. "You're a sorceress, aren't you? You're Mistress Seela."

"I am," she admitted. "And you are Kwil, and she's Nera."

Nera stopped in her tracks. "How do you know who we are?"

Laughing softly, Seela replied, "Don't worry, young one. I can sense much about you. How else do you think I knew to come to your rescue?"

"You can read our thoughts?" Kwil asked.

"Not exactly," Seela replied. "But I can read the intention of your heart. I know you have come seeking knowledge."

Kwil glanced over at Nera, attempting to contain his excitement. They wouldn't have to explain the situation or convince this woman to trust them. Through her magic, she already knew everything.

"You must be sure of yourself," Nera whispered to Kwil. "If she senses any self-doubt, she might not want to teach you. Let her see only your confidence."

"I'll try," he whispered back.

"Damn imps," Seela said as she stepped inside. Beckoning for the two to follow, she added, "They know to stay a hundred yards from my cabin. Disgusting creatures."

"No offense, Madam, but why don't you remain in your larger size?" Nera asked. "It must be safer that way."

Hopping onto a stool, Seela replied, "I'm more agile in this form." Grinning at Kwil, she said, "Plus I'm less imposing."

"I think I prefer this form as well," Kwil remarked. She was certainly less terrifying as a small cat. Her panther form was terrifying, even when she was on his side.

Seela jumped onto the table at the center of the room, delicately striding between the vials and flasks that left little spare room for movement. Searching through the labels, she selected the appropriate antidote and placed her paw on the stopper. "This is the one," she said.

Kwil lifted the bottle and looked it over. It was an ordinary gray liquid with no apparent magical properties. "Do I drink it?" he asked.

"Not unless you want to vomit," Seela replied. "Place it on a cloth and hold it against your wound. You'll be good as new in minutes."

The young man did as she said, placing a few drops of the gray tincture onto a strip of cloth. Pressing it against the bite wound, he immediately felt the soothing effects of the medicine. Glancing around the cabin, he noticed several shelves filled with colorful tinctures. "Why do you have so many potions?" he wondered aloud. He immediately regretted the question, hoping he hadn't offended the woman whose help he required. "I'm sorry," he said. "I don't mean to pry."

Waving a dismissive paw, she replied, "When one lives alone, one must be prepared for any scenario." Grinning, she added, "And I enjoy dabbling in potions and creating my own concoctions. It's certainly a fun way to pass a rainy day."

"Why do you live alone?" Nera asked. "You're a Feles. You could be wealthy, famous, and admired all over Gi'gata." In fact, Seela had given up what Nera was seeking. Though she didn't care to be rich, she wanted to make music that people would flock to hear. Bringing joy to a crowd through song was all she'd ever desired.

"Had I been born of a different color, I could have had that life," Seela replied. "A solid black Feles is an ill omen among our people. A superstition exists that we are bringers of bad fortune, and that simply looking upon us can invite evil into a person's life."

"Because of your color?" Kwil asked, shocked. He understood prejudice well, being born of the lowest class possible. But prejudice against a Gatan was unknown to him. Why would they turn against one of their own?

"I've seen Gatans with black pelts before," Nera stated. "They weren't treated any differently."

"In this day and age that is true," Seela replied. "But a Feles is not an ordinary Gatan." Looking at Nera with scolding eyes, she said, "You obviously haven't studied ancient history. Our ancestors were violent and cruel, sacrificing those who were black of pelt."

Nera gasped. "I didn't know," she said. She felt even more ashamed of her own people. How could they do something so cruel to their own kind?

"Don't get me wrong," Seela went on. "Being sacrificed to the gods was considered an honor. Kits with black fur were offered up by their own parents, and they were blessed for it. At least they thought they were. Over time, the practice ended, and the attitude toward black-furred Gatans turned sour. We were reviled, accused of practicing dark magic, and sent into exile."

"How long ago was this?" Kwil asked. "Were your people still four-legged?"

"Yes," Seela replied. "That was the time when everyone was a Feles. Now the prejudice remains against only those who are like me. One in a million births produces a Feles, and most of those are of an

212

acceptable color. It is my misfortune, and my greatest honor, to be born this way."

"You enjoy solitude?" Kwil asked, wondering if she preferred the life she had to that of an average Gatan.

"I am not alone," Seela replied. "I have the creatures of the forest. They raised me and shared their knowledge of the arcane. I have only a few close friends, but they are quite dear to me. I wouldn't give them up for anything, not even the chance to live among my people."

Reaching up to remove the cloth from Kwil's wound, Seela smiled. "It's healed," she announced.

Kwil ran his fingers over the bite and felt nothing. "It's completely gone," he said. Not only spells could work great feats of magic; potions could do that as well. Never before had he considered making potions, but now he was eager to learn. "Mistress Seela," he began, "would you teach me your craft? Master Rili was forced to send me away, and he said I should seek you out. I wish with all my heart to serve as your apprentice."

A warm smile graced the Feles' lips. "I'd be delighted," she said. "I see great things in you, Kwil." Glancing at Nera, she said, "I see great things in you as well. You are both welcome to stay and learn."

"I don't wish to learn magic," Nera replied. "But I thank you for the kind offer."

"Are you leaving?" Kwil asked, hoping she would stay, but knowing her dreams would take her elsewhere.

"I don't think I can learn music here," she said, avoiding Kwil's gaze. The sadness in his eyes was difficult for her to look at. "I'll have to find a troupe somewhere."

Seela shook her head. "There is much this forest can teach you of music," she said. "You should stay at least a short time to see what it has to offer."

Intrigued by the suggestion, Nera agreed. "I will," she said. Maybe it would be easier to leave after Kwil was settled in and his lessons had begun.

"So," Seela began, "Rili sent you to me. How is he anyway?"

"He's doing well," Kwil replied. "He said you were his teacher."

"Indeed," she replied. "I taught him many years ago when he was just a young kit. He was eager and bright but a little full of himself. I suppose he still is. He hasn't visited me in years."

"Was Rili afraid of you?" Nera wondered. After all, he was a model student and had to have known the superstitions surrounding the black Feles.

"Not for a moment," Seela replied. "He wasn't allowed to learn magic at the College. He was of low birth, and his parents could not afford the tuition. There was no one else to teach him. The look of his teacher mattered not. It was the lessons he wanted, regardless of who was teaching them." Chuckling, she added, "It was rather fun having him around back then." Her golden eyes grew nostalgic as she remembered the eager young student she once taught. She saw many similarities in Kwil.

"You should be proud of him," Nera said. "Not only is he a master wizard, he also helps escaped slaves return to their homelands."

"I would expect no less," Seela replied. "And I am proud of him."

"Can we start my lessons now?" Kwil asked, eager to get started. Every corner of the cabin reminded him of magic, its presence emanating from the walls. With the poison out of his system, he could sense great power here, and he craved the knowledge of its creator. Seela's golden eyes spoke of magic far beyond anything he had sensed from Rili. This was where he truly belonged, and he was ready to begin his lessons.

"In the morning," Seela replied. "First you need rest."

"Agreed," Nera said. "I, for one, could use a bath and some clean clothes."

Disappointed, Kwil remained silent. Yes, he was dirty and needed a bath as well, but delaying his lessons by one night was physically painful to him.

Seela led her guests upstairs and pointed to two doors. "You may use these rooms," she said. "The bath water heats itself," she added with a grin. Retiring to her own room, she left the visitors to their rest.

Nera could sense Kwil's disappointment. "It's only one night," she said. "After tomorrow, you'll be on your way to becoming a master wizard, and no one will come looking for you here." After hearing Seela's account of history, Nera knew no Gatan would set foot anywhere near the cabin. Attitudes did not change quickly in this land, and no one would risk being cursed by an evil Feles. The thought brought a smile to Nera's lips. Seela was possibly the most intriguing person she'd met. Despite being an outcast, she appeared to live life on her own terms and was genuinely happy. She was free from the rules of society and master of her own destiny. One day, Nera hoped to have the same thing.

Chapter 16

After a hot bath and a full night's rest, Nera awoke feeling more alive than she ever had. The forest air was fresh and inviting, despite the darkness of the landscape. Looking out her bedroom window, she could see only beauty. The dark trees and withered leaves held a sense of mystery, no longer one of foreboding and fear.

Pulling the last of her clean clothing from her bag, she silently hoped Kwil would learn a spell to wash laundry without having to get wet. It was cold, and she had no desire to stand outside scrubbing. After dressing, she retrieved her lute and headed downstairs.

Seela was already up, a breakfast of fruit and nuts waiting at the edge of the table. Despite having guests, she had not bothered to tidy up. Vials and flasks were strewn about the kitchen, leaving little room for cooking and eating.

"Good morning," Nera said, announcing her presence.

"Good morning to you," Seela replied. "I trust you slept well?"

"Better than I can remember," Nera said, taking an apple from the basket. "Would it be all right if I sat outside to play?"

"Oh yes," Seela said. "The imps are gone, and no one will bother you." She headed to the window and pushed it open. "If you sit here, I'll be able to hear your music."

Nera beamed with pride. Seela hadn't heard her play a single note, yet she was willing to lend her ears. Nera hoped she'd be pleasantly surprised by her talent. Stepping outside, she took in a deep gulp of forest air and let it out slowly. No more stuffy towns or noble manor houses would be in her future. She would play for a traveling company, giving concerts under the stars.

Taking up a position near the window, she fiddled momentarily with her strings to make sure they were in tune. Then, she strummed softly, humming along with the rhythm.

"Why don't you sing?" Seela's voice called from inside.

Pausing in her song, Nera replied, "I'm afraid I don't have that gift."

"Nonsense," the Feles said. "You can learn. You simply need a teacher."

"Would that be you?" Nera asked, grinning.

"I'm afraid not," Seela replied. "I never took the time to learn, but I do have a friend who might be able to help. I'll try to get in touch with her."

Nera returned to her song, playing with her eyes closed. When she opened her eyes, she thought she saw movement among the trees. Peering into the woods, she saw nothing and dismissed it as her imagination. Switching her song to a lively tune, she tapped her foot to keep time. As she stared into the trees, she was certain she saw something buzzing around. Standing, she took a few steps toward the trees for a closer look.

Two tiny figures appeared before her eyes. "Play more!" they shouted with high voices.

Nera's jaw dropped open. They looked exactly like the pixies she had seen in stories as a young kit. Saying nothing, she lifted her lute and continued the music. The pixies darted and dipped, dancing along with the rhythm. Nera laughed to herself, hardly able to believe what was happening. Here among the ominous trees of the Dark Forest were creatures straight out of a fairy tale. She made a note to tell Kwil his scary stories of the forest couldn't possibly be true, at least not in the vicinity of Seela's cabin.

As she finished her song, the pixies came forward to applaud before buzzing away into the trees. Inspired by the enchanted beings, she sat down to begin a new composition. Attempting to capture their flight pattern by song, she plucked at her strings until she found the correct notes. It was still a work in progress, but it was coming along.

Seated at her desk near the window, Seela tapped her tail to the music. "Sounds like the forest is having an effect," she called to Nera.

Nera smiled. "I think you're right," she replied.

* * * * *

Kwil did not wake until late that morning, the sound of Nera's song greeting him as his eyes finally opened. He stretched his arms and sat up, certain that it was the best night's sleep he'd ever had. The bed was extremely comfortable, almost as if it had been made specifically to fit his body. The thought gave him pause, and he ran his hand along the mattress to examine it. Smiling, he realized the mattress had indeed conformed to him. It was enchanted, as were most items in the home, he suspected. Seela had an extraordinary talent for magic, and Kwil couldn't wait to start learning.

Jumping out of the bed, he ran to the door and opened it. The cool breeze reminded him that he had yet to dress, and he quickly shut the door to ready himself for the day. The sun was shining straight through the window, and he noticed its high position. He had slept much later than intended. Half the morning was already gone, and he had not reported to his mistress.

Combing his hair, he tried to tame his dark locks into an orderly fashion. Splashing water over his face, he was pleasantly surprised to find it warm. After dressing, he headed down the stairs to greet the others.

"Look who's finally out of bed," Seela jibed. She had taken the extra time to clear the table and neatly organize her potions inside the cupboard.

"Forgive me," Kwil said. "I must have been more tired than I thought."

"Here," Seela said, filling a wooden bowl with porridge. "Eat."

"I'm not all that hungry," Kwil replied. His zeal for learning had usurped his appetite.

"Nonsense," Seela said. "You can't learn on an empty stomach. Eat now and then we will begin."

Nera paused in her playing to peek inside the window. Kwil was busily shoving spoonfuls of porridge into his mouth, and Seela was admiring her work with the potions. Staying silent, Nera decided to hold her position and observe them. Kwil's first lesson with Seela would probably be amusing to watch. It might even inspire a song.

"All finished," Kwil announced, swallowing the last mouthful.

"Very well," Seela replied. "Let's begin."

Striding over to Kwil, Seela took the bowl from his hands. Spreading silver magic over it, the dish became clean as Kwil watched.

"You have to teach me that spell," he said.

"Later," she replied. "That is not today's lesson." Extending her paw, she handed the bowl back to him. "Do you feel the magic in this bowl?"

Taking the bowl, Kwil placed his hands on either side and closed his eyes. He felt a faint trace of magic still in the wood. "I think so," he stated.

"Good," she replied. "Now draw it out."

Wrinkling his brow, he opened an eye to look at his mistress. "I don't know how," he admitted. He had felt magic in the stone he used against the cockatrice, but it had never occurred to him that he might take the magic inside it for his own. "What is the incantation?" he asked.

"There is none," she replied. "This is a spell you cast by being in contact with an object. If it contains magic, you can claim it. Now focus your mind and do as I told you."

His mistress sounded impatient, so Kwil closed his eyes and tried to reach into the magical residue left on the bowl. Imagining himself reaching between the grains of the wood, he attempted to steal the magic inside. He tried until his hands began to shake, but he failed to retrieve the magic. He still sensed its presence locked inside the bowl. Opening his eyes, he stared blankly at Seela.

"All of us have our shortcomings, and no one has limitless power," she explained. "Only an elemental is replenished by its element. The rest of us must find it where we can." She took the bowl from his hands and spread red magic over it. "Try it now," she said.

Undeterred, Kwil made another attempt. This time, he could feel the heat of the magic against his hands, and he called to it with his mind. Magic oozed from the wood, his fingers taking on a red hue in response. A strong sensation of heat filled his chest as the magic became his own. His eyes opened wide, he looked up at Seela. "I did it," he announced, stunned by his achievement.

"Good," she replied. "You managed it on the second element. Now we know your affinity is for fire."

"Does that mean I'll be a fire mage?" he wondered.

"If that is the path you choose," she replied. "You may learn from any school: air, fire, water, or earth. But most humans and Gatans take the time to master only one."

"Could I master them all?" he asked, his mind swimming with the possibilities.

"You could," she replied. "But it will take many long years of study. Perhaps more than a lifetime."

He thought for a moment and said, "I'll master fire first, and then I'll master as many as I can before I die."

"Most are content to master one," Seela replied. "After that, they consider themselves wise enough."

Shaking his head, he replied, "I wish never to stop learning. There will always be knowledge out there that I don't possess, and I want to find as much of it as I can."

A smile crept across Seela's face. "You are wise for someone so young," she said.

Curious, he asked, "What element are you mistress of?"

"Air," she replied. "And earth. I am studying water now."

"Maybe I can help you with fire," he responded. "That is, if you don't master it on your own first." He wasn't sure whether he had misspoke.

Seela laughed. "If you master fire before I finish with water, then I will gladly accept your help," she said. "I may have you bested now, but in time, you may become the more powerful one."

Kwil doubted that, but he didn't say so. He wasn't even sure how to know when he had mastered any element to move on to another. How do you master something when there is always more to learn? Though he might finish the lessons and earn the title, he would not stop studying. There would always be more for him to learn, and with Seela as his guide, he might learn more than he'd ever imagined.

"Come now," Seela said, opening the cabin door. "You must learn to draw magic from a creature."

They stepped outside together, Kwil's expression displaying his uncertainty. What creature did she have in mind? Would he be fighting those imps again? He hadn't had much success the last time, but he would do as he was told.

Seela trotted over to a tree where a small brown spider was wrapping up an ant that had caught itself in her web. She whispered a few words to the creature, but Kwil could not hear her reply.

Returning with the spider resting on her head, Seela said, "This lovely young lady has agreed to help us with the lesson." Lifting her paw, the spider climbed onto it. The Feles spread white magic over the spider, the eight-legged creature trembling in response. Seela leaned an ear toward the spider. "She says that tickled," she said before passing the spider to Kwil.

Kwil took the spider in the palm of his hand and did his best to hide his discomfort. "Does this work the same as the bowl?" he asked. He had no desire to harm the little volunteer.

"It does," Seela said. "But this is not a fire spell because I would not harm this creature. Be gentle with her, but be sound in your resolve." After a pause, she said, "And take your time."

Barely able to feel the spider on his hand, Kwil wasn't sure he would be able to draw magic from her. Closing his eyes, he attempted to block out all distractions. Focusing his mind to the spider's magic, he found it almost impossible to detect. Seela had put only a small amount into the creature, forcing Kwil to work to find it.

Holding his concentration, Kwil managed to sense the presence of a slight amount of magic. Directing all his energy to the spider, he realized he could feel her tiny feet against the palm of his hand. There was a slight warmth to them, but he did not know whether it was her warmth or his own. Realizing it didn't matter, he saw the opportunity to draw out the magic. It passed through the spider's body, exiting through her feet and leaving a faint glow of white on Kwil's palm.

Opening his eyes, he could have sworn he saw the spider grin at him. The magic passed into his body, giving him a tingling sensation in his veins. White magic was used for healing, and it revitalized him as it added itself to his magical stores.

"Well done," Seela said. "And thank you, Miss Arachnid."

The spider lowered herself on a thin string of silk and scurried away.

"You've done well for your first try absorbing magic from another creature," Seela said, a hint of pride in her voice. "That would have come in useful against those imps. Had you drained one, you would have found him quite docile."

"I'll keep that in mind," Kwil replied.

"With more practice, you'll perfect your technique and be able to perform this spell much more easily." With a flash of gold in her eyes, she cast an energy burst at one of the trees, lighting it with a golden hue. Then she cast silver and green at various limbs and leaves. "That should keep you busy for a while," she said. "Oh, and this too." Spinning around, she cast white magic at Nera, who had been observing the entire time.

The blast hit the Gatan in her midsection, and she jumped in surprise. She was unhurt, but a little annoyed at being used as a guinea pig. At least the spider had given permission first. She crossed her arms and stood still, waiting for Kwil to practice his skills.

Seela laughed and headed back toward the cabin. "See how you do with absorbing those spells," she instructed him. "You might want to start with Nera first. She looks a bit perturbed." Chuckling, she stepped inside and prepared to close the door.

"Wait," Kwil said. "How long do you want me to keep practicing?"

"That's a silly question," Seela replied. "You keep practicing until you can't do it anymore." Closing the door behind her, she left her apprentice to study on his own.

Though he'd never practiced magic until his stores were depleted, Kwil was willing to try. It would be the first time he'd experienced the sensation, having read about it numerous times. Each wizard's experience could vary slightly, but it mostly involved fatigue and, naturally, the inability to cast any spells.

Approaching Nera, he kept his head low. "Sorry," he said. "I didn't want her to use you for my lessons."

"Let's just get this over with," Nera said with a huff. The white magic had not harmed her. In fact, it gave her an energetic feeling.

Laying his hands on Nera's shoulders, Kwil closed his eyes and focused his mind to his friend. Magic radiated all through her, and he could hear the faint sounds of her lute, though she was not playing. Pulling the magic from inside her, he transferred it into himself. He could feel the magic add itself to his stores, but he did not experience any strange sensation. Removing his hands from her shoulders, he realized it had taken a good deal of his own magic to pull power away from her. He had used more than he had gained. "Fascinating," he said.

Nera only shook her head and picked up her lute. "I'll be over here if you need me, but don't cast any spells my direction."

Nodding, Kwil moved away to focus on the tree. Its golden magic shone so brightly, it had a hypnotic effect on him. He had never even read about gold magic. Placing his hands on the trunk, he attempted to absorb its power, but each time he felt it enter his body, it flew out again. Apparently, the spell was self-sustaining. No wonder Seela had told him to practice until he ran out. Smiling to himself, he decided to drain the limbs and leaves first, and then return to work on the tree. It was going to be a long day.

Chapter 17

Kwil awoke feeling more alive than ever. A fire was lit in his belly, his magical stores being completely replenished as he slept. He had feared the drained feeling would stay with him much longer, or that he would require a potion to replace the magic he had spent. To his surprise, that hadn't been the case. He felt magic within himself greater than it had ever been.

After readying himself for the day, he made his way downstairs to find the cabin empty. The sound of Nera's lute let him know that she was around, likely sitting outside. Opening the door, he stepped out into the chilly winter and took in a deep breath. The air smelled of dried leaves and fresh soil.

"Good morning," Nera said upon seeing her friend.

"Good morning," he echoed.

Seela was perched on a low limb, her paws crossed in front of her. "How are you feeling this morning?" she asked, wondering how he had responded to the magical drain.

"I feel wonderful," he replied, still sounding surprised.

"Looks like we can start our lesson then," Seela replied, jumping down from the tree. "I thought the three of us might take a little walk this morning. There is a suitable place for the next spell I want to teach you."

Kwil and Nera gladly followed Seela as she led them deeper into the forest. It was silent all around, no animals scurrying or shrieks in the distance. The Dark Forest's reputation as a place of evil was quickly being disproved.

His curiosity getting the better of him, Kwil moved beside his mistress to ask some questions. "Mistress," he began, "I was wondering about yesterday's lesson."

"What about it?"

"Well, you had me draw magic from both the spider and Nera. I'm curious why you didn't have me try to absorb magic from you."

"Simple," she responded. "Because it wouldn't have worked, not yet anyway. You can perform the spell only on sorcerers who are not as powerful as you. A test of wills, if you prefer to think of it that way. Most will resist you, but as you progress, you'll find you're able to tackle more-difficult opponents."

"Do you see me fighting many?" he asked.

"Yes," she replied bluntly. "You will fight all your life from now on."

The young mage didn't like the sound of that. He wanted only to perform good things with his magic, not bring harm to others. "I don't wish to fight," he said. "I want to help people with my magic."

Seela replied, "You will help many, and you will see that justice is done. To do that you will have to fight. There is no other way."

"Surely peace can resolve all things," he said. How could fighting bring about peace?

"Some things cannot be resolved peacefully," she replied. "For example, slavery. You won't talk the Gatans into giving up their slaves."

Kwil paused in his walking.

Seela paused as well. "It's sad but true," she said. "You will have to fight for this."

"And you see me being the person to bring about this change?" Kwil couldn't believe this was his destiny. Of all people, why would this fall to him? He was no one, and he had no position in society. No one was going to listen to him.

"I do," she said, "with Nera at your side." Glancing back at the girl, she said, "Keep your friend close. She is a part of your destiny. Remember that should you ever become cross with her. You mustn't let anything come in the way of your friendship. Without her, all is lost."

"I will remember," he replied, his voice barely louder than a whisper. The warning was prophetic, and he would keep it with him always. It was a heavy burden to lay at his feet, but if he could someday make a difference for other slaves, then he had to try. For now, he hoped the days of fighting were far away. He couldn't even fight off the imp, so an army of Gatans was out of the question.

Nera overheard the conversation but said nothing. Having her destiny intertwined with Kwil's would explain her reasons for not wanting to leave his side just yet. There was so much music she could learn if only she had the courage to go out on her own. But something had made her reluctant to go, and she was enjoying seeing Kwil learn. Not to mention, the forest was a perfect place to study music, as Seela had suggested.

Nera had no idea how she could help Kwil end slavery, but it was a subject dear to her heart. It was wrong to own other people, no matter how the Gatans tried to justify it. If there was the tiniest chance she could help put an end to it, she would postpone her musical dream to make it happen.

Seela continued the march, seemingly unchanged by the conversation. Despite knowing him only a few days, she could see many things in Kwil's future. She was proud to have him as her student.

"I have another question," he said.

"Of course you do," she replied. "An inquisitive mind is the mark of a true scholar."

He decided to take those words as a compliment. There would be hundreds or thousands more questions to come throughout his lessons. He was glad to find Seela receptive to them. "Have my magical stores increased since yesterday?" he asked. "I feel different somehow."

"Yes, they have," she replied. "And that is the perfect spell to practice if you want to increase them further. The more you practice any magic, the larger those stores will grow. To a point, at least."

"So there's a limit?" he wondered.

"As far as I know, yes," she stated.

237

"And sleeping will restore it all," he continued. "Whenever my stores are depleted, all I need do is sleep?"

Seela stopped in her tracks. "Humans require potions to replenish their stores," she informed him.

"Apparently not," he replied with a smile. He had taken no potion, and he felt in perfect shape.

Seela shook her head. "You are not fully human," she said. "You have elven ancestry. I can see it."

Unable to believe his ears, Kwil stood in stunned silence, gaping at his mistress.

"That's why magic comes naturally to you," Nera said, moving to his side. "That actually explains a lot." Elves learned magic far more readily than humans or Gatans. She had never met an elf before, and now she was standing next to one.

"I can't be an elf," he said.

"One of your parents, I suspect your mother, has elven ancestry," Seela replied. "You are more human than elf, but the elf is there, without a doubt." With a flash of gold in her eyes, she blasted energy at a pile of leaves, sending them flying high into the air. "What did you notice about that spell?" she asked.

After thinking for a moment, he said, "You did not speak an incantation as I would have. Also, you required no finger movements. How is that possible?"

"I am not like other Gatans," she replied. "You have learned from Gatan books and read tales of other lands that gave you little to no information about true magic." She lifted her paw for him to observe. "I have no fingers to perform those delicate movements of Gatan magic, yet I am unhindered. The same is true for you. You don't need to learn those movements, nor do you need to speak an incantation."

"Because of my ancestry?"

"Exactly," she said. "Let the magic be a part of you, and it will manifest itself. All you need do is visualize it."

This was a whole new way of performing spells, one that he had never imagined. Far beyond the techniques he had read in Nera's schoolbooks, Seela's method was a new challenge for him. This was the magic of a true master.

"This isn't magic that can be taught," Seela continued. "This is innate, and it is far beyond what most Gatans or humans will experience. Your heritage has given you the key to something amazing." Her golden eyes gleamed as she looked upon her student.

Rili had not had such talent, and Seela was delighted to have one such as Kwil as her apprentice. She could teach him things that other students could not learn.

Now more than ever, Kwil was eager to learn about his heritage and the parents he never knew. What land had they come from? Were all of its inhabitants wizards? He'd never read of such a place, but maybe it existed. He doubted he would be special there. All of the inhabitants were probably capable of magic, it just depended on how hard they studied. Still, he was burning with the desire to know them. But he was far from ready to leave Seela's side. Now was the time to learn all he could and hone his skills. There was so much yet to do.

They pressed on through the woods in silence, their feet cutting a path among the fallen leaves. The winter air was still and felt warmer as they went, proceeding into the darker corners of the forest. After nearly half an hour, Seela paused and announced they had reached their destination.

Kwil and Nera exchanged glances. Ahead of them stood the strangest trees either of them had ever seen. They were excessively wide with smooth bark the color of charcoal. Thin strips of various colors dripped vertically down the trunks, as if someone had spilled paint down them from on high.

Nera approached one of the trees and ran her hand over its bark. Her mouth gaping open, she stood entranced by its beauty. As her hand remained on the trunk, a song came into her mind. Its notes changed swiftly, the song of the tree playing over and over in her head. Her heart swelled with emotions: happiness, sadness, love, and despair. All of these sights the tree had seen in its expansive lifetime. For millennia it had stood here, witnessing the passage of time and those who came before. Overwhelmed, Nera dropped to her knees, her hand releasing from the bark. The music stopped, allowing her time to collect herself.

"It's most intense the first time you encounter them," Seela said, coming to the girl's side. Placing a gentle paw on her back, she said, "Listen to them. Hear the stories they have to tell, and learn from them. They will show you music you never imagined."

Nera nodded slowly, turning her attention back to the tree. Studying the colors running down the bark, she felt the music without touching the tree. There was great power here, and though she was not a creature of magic, she could feel it throughout her body. Gathering her courage, she placed her hand against the bark once more, determined to listen as long as she could.

Visions of elves and ancients passed through her mind, the songs of their people playing softly in her ears. Tears filled her eyes as she witnessed their leaving, never to be seen in this land again. The trees mourned their passing, many of them desiring to join the elves in their eternity. But here they stayed, a part of the world that could never be undone. Here they would stay until all came to an end.

Sitting back on her heels, Nera took a moment to rest. She felt weary and desired sleep, but Seela would not allow it. Laying a paw on the girl's hand, her eyes flashed with gold. The magic spread over Nera, renewing her strength and removing all trace of fatigue.

Nera smiled at the Feles as she studied her golden eyes. Before her stood a creature who truly cared for her. Here in the wilderness, with Kwil and Seela, she was home.

Kwil touched the bark of the tree as well, witnessing the passage of time as the trees had seen it. The magic of the elves pierced his soul, increasing his desire to know more about his ancestors. Were these his people? The trees could not tell. But the magic they possessed and their indomitable spirit had left a mark on this place.

"If you've finished for now, I have a lesson for you," Seela announced.

"Of course," Kwil replied, straightening his shirt.

"Sometimes you will not be able to fight your way through a situation, no matter how powerful you are," she began. "If you are to survive, you must learn how to pass through these situations unscathed. One way is to alter your state."

"You mean change what I am? My physical form?" he asked.

"Indeed," she replied. "You have touched the trees and formed a bond, at least for a time. Now I want you to mimic them. Alter yourself to match their bark. If you do this correctly, you will be undetectable."

"What is the incantation?" Kwil asked, eager to try it.

"There is none," she said. "You must visualize this to make it happen. Use your magic and your mind. Leave your fingers still and your voice silent."

Drawing in a deep breath, Kwil prepared himself for his first attempt. His fingers twitched slightly out of habit, but he steadied them and focused his mind to the trees. Staring at the colors before him, he could feel them entering his body. With his full concentration, he allowed the colors inside him and projected them throughout his form.

"You're doing well," Seela encouraged him. "Hold onto it."

Kwil's mind swam with colors, the magic moving over his body. A faint glint of gold flashed in his eyes, but he did not waver. Holding onto the spell, he forced the colors to obey him, his clothing taking on the hue of the trees.

Nera clasped a hand to her mouth to cut off a laugh. As she watched, Kwil's clothing seemed to disappear, blending in with the tree behind him. The disappearance of sections of his body was more amusing than she had anticipated, but she remained quiet, hoping not to interrupt his practice.

"Good, good, keep going," Seela urged him.

Kwil finally allowed his eyes to close, the image of the tree burned into his memory. His thoughts transferred to his skin, and he visualized it changing to his will. As he stood in place, he became part of the tree, his own physical appearance melding with the bark.

Nera watched in awe as her friend disappeared before her eyes. Her jaw dropped slightly, her eyes not budging from the spot where Kwil had stood. Only knowing that Seela was nearby stopped her from panicking. Would he be able to break the spell on his own? Had he truly disappeared? As she continued to stare, she noticed the lines on the trees moving slightly. It was Kwil's chest rising and falling as he breathed deeply, attempting to hold the spell.

"Bravo!" Seela shouted, leaping in the air.

Nera jumped to her feet cheering as well. As she moved toward the tree, Kwil reappeared, his face beaming.

"I actually did it!" he said. He couldn't believe the magic had worked. Without an incantation or finger movements, he had succeeded in casting his most difficult spell to date. He looked over at Seela, gratitude in his eyes. This was her doing. Her presence and guidance had made this possible.

"Well done," she said. Clearing her throat, she added, "We must celebrate our victories, but we must not dwell there. Now keep practicing."

Kwil resumed his practice, blending in with leaves, trees, and bare earth. Each attempt seemed more difficult, and he felt himself draining of magic more quickly than before. After two hours, he was completely spent and collapsed on the forest floor.

Seela took sympathy on him and lent him some magic through the touch of her paw. "That will get you home, at least," she said, chuckling.

Exhausted but undaunted, Kwil climbed to his feet. He approached Nera, who had fallen asleep at the base of one of the painted trees, and shook her gently. "Time to go," he said.

"Yes, yes," Seela said. "Rest up, freshen up, and be ready to meet a friend of mine tonight." She trotted off toward the cabin, her tail held high.

Chapter 18

With sunset looming, Seela set about preparing dinner for her guest, who had yet to arrive. There was much to be done, but with the help of magic and a house full of enchanted items, the work would be much easier.

"Do you need any help?" Kwil asked, eager to lend a second pair of hands to the task. He had napped away the afternoon, and his magic was restored and ready for use.

"Certainly," Seela replied. This would be a good opportunity for him to continue his practice.

"I'll help too," Nera offered, stepping inside the kitchen.

"That won't be necessary," Seela stated. "But you can play us some music while we work."

Happy to oblige, Nera ran upstairs to fetch her lute. Returning moments later, she plopped down in a chair at the table and strummed in time with Seela's magic.

With a wave of her paw and a flash of gold, Seela kneaded the dough for two loaves of bread and set them aside to rise. "Speed that up for me, apprentice," she said, turning her attention to the vegetables.

Kwil stared at the bread, knowing that heat would decrease its rising time. But too much heat too soon would kill the yeast, and they'd end up with a hardened mess. *There must be a trick to this,* he thought. Glancing over at Seela, he marveled at her abilities. She used no knife, instead turning to magic to peel and slice potatoes and carrots. Kwil had no idea how to perform such a spell. He could make them fly through the air at his command, but he couldn't manipulate them as his mistress could.

After staring blankly at the bread, an idea occurred to him. He could concentrate on only the bits of yeast, adding his magic to them. Bending them to his will, he would have the bread to the correct size in no time. Spreading his hands over the loaves, he reminded himself not to move his fingers. His lips moved slightly as he mouthed an incantation, but no sound could be heard. Old habits were hard to break, but he was making every effort to conform to Seela's wishes. Concentrating on the bread, he held his breath as it rose to double its size in a matter of seconds.

Lifting the pans, Kwil scanned the kitchen for the oven. To his surprise, he found none. "Where's the oven?" he asked, surprised that he had not noticed earlier.

"I don't need one," Seela replied, a mischievous smile on her lips. "I have a fire apprentice." She swatted him once on the arm as she passed by, her thoughts moving on to the venison roast.

Kwil sat the pans back on the table and took in a deep breath. Moving his hands in a circular pattern, he summoned the heat within himself.

"Uh-uh," Seela said, wagging a paw at him. "That's not the way I taught you."

The stare of his mistress's golden eyes embarrassed him. "Right," he said, placing his arms down at his side. Closing his eyes, he visualized the bread in his mind, all the while conjuring heat within himself. He imagined the bread cooking through, the crust browning to perfection. Drinking in the scent of fresh bread, he could not resist opening his eyes. Before him were two browned loaves.

"Well done," Seela said with an approving nod. "Now cook the roast."

Taking the pot from his mistress, he said, "You know, I never saw myself as much of a cook."

"It's much easier with magic," Seela replied. "If it doesn't taste right, you can simply change it. Failing that, you can change your dinner guests' opinions of the food." She laughed softly to herself and returned to her work.

Serenaded by Nera's song, the dinner preparations seemed to fly by. Eventually, the variety of scents became too much for the musician to bear. "I hope your friend arrives soon," she said. "I'm starving, and smelling all this is torture."

Kwil considered slicing a piece of bread for her but thought better of it. Seela wanted everything to be perfect for her friend. Instead, he tossed Nera an apple.

"Finish setting the table!" Seela shouted. "She's here!"

Kwil rushed to make sure all the plates and silverware were out, and Nera wiggled the cork free from a bottle of wine. Seela went to the door to greet her guest.

"Welcome!" she called out the door. As the woman stepped inside, she introduced her guests to one another. "This is Kwil and Nera," she said, indicating each of them in turn. "I'd like you both to meet Aqualia."

Before them stood a captivating woman, her skin deeply tanned by the sun. Her pale eyes and sea foam green hair that cascaded down her back gave her a striking appearance. Kwil could hardly take his eyes off her. In all his days, he could not remember encountering anyone so breathtaking.

As Aqualia passed by to take her seat, Kwil continued to stare. Seela flashed a cutting glance his direction, demanding that he get his eyes back in his head. As if coming out of a daze, he obeyed, blinking to remove the image.

"It's lovely to meet you," Nera said, still clutching her lute.

"You're a musician?" Aqualia asked.

"I am," Nera responded proudly.

"Then you must play for us after dinner," Aqualia said. "I'd love to hear your music."

"My friend here is a Siren," Seela informed the others. "She has the most beautiful voice you've ever heard."

Nera's mouth hung open a moment. She could already hear the music from Aqualia's lips, and she was intrigued. "Will you sing for us?" she asked.

"Certainly," the Siren promised.

"If I can persuade her to stay awhile, I intend to ask her if she's willing to assist you in your voice training." Seela looked expectantly at her friend.

"I'd be delighted to help this young lady unlock her talents," Aqualia said, her face lighting up.

"It's settled then," Seela said. "I've already prepared a room for you."

"Lovely," the Siren replied. "I'll be able to stay only a few days, but I'm looking forward to it."

"Shall we eat?" Seela asked, gesturing a paw at the table. All the foods they had prepared were laid out before them, their aromas enticing the group to dine.

Kwil poured wine for everyone, lingering a bit longer at Aqualia's glass. There was something mystical and intriguing about her, and he could sense an unseen magic. Feeling it would be impolite to ask, he remained silent, trying to solve the mystery on his own. He had never read about Sirens, and now he regretted it. At first light, he would search Seela's library for the information he craved.

Aqualia charmed the others with talk of her homeland—a tiny island on the sea, inhabited by her and her sisters, where every day was sunny and sweet. Of course that wasn't truly the case, but Aqualia would not mention dark days or stormy seas. This was a night to make merry, and she had no desire to darken the mood.

"I would love to see your island one day," Nera said, leaning her head on her hand. "It sounds amazing."

"Then you should visit," Aqualia replied. "Once your duties here permit it."

"She has no duties," Seela remarked. "She's free to come and go as she likes. Only Kwil is bound to me. Unless, of course, he chooses to end his apprenticeship."

Kwil found himself tongue-tied by the suggestion and crammed a piece of bread in his mouth to avoid a reply. The twinkle in his mistress's eye suggested she was only kidding. Both she and Kwil knew that he would never choose to abandon his studies.

"Tell us how the two of you met," Nera begged. "It must be a fascinating encounter.

"Do I tell it or you?" Aqualia asked, facing Seela.

"You start, I'll finish," Seela replied.

"Well, I had hoped to keep the conversation light...." Aqualia paused for a moment. "Well, let's just say I wasn't having a very good day. I was swimming alongside a ship, and the men were admiring me as usual. Then out of nowhere, there was an explosion. Splintered wood flew everywhere, a few pieces striking me as I tried to get out of the way. I was bleeding heavily and in a lot of pain."

"What caused the explosion?" Kwil asked.

"I have no idea," she replied, shaking her head. "The ship must have been hauling dangerous cargo, but I never saw it, and nothing remained of it afterward."

"How did you manage to get to safety?" Nera asked, her brow wrinkled in concern.

"I managed to pull myself onto a tiny islet, despite the searing pain in my back. I had a rather large gash, not to mention dozens of scrapes and bruises. I laid there all night, drifting in and out of consciousness. When I saw a small black figure coming toward me, I thought I was hallucinating."

"Couldn't you use magic to summon help?" Nera asked. "Sirens have magic in their voices, don't they?"

"We do indeed," she replied. "But I hadn't the strength, and my voice wouldn't carry across the waves."

Ready to tell her part of the story, Seela cleared her throat. "First, you need to understand why I was in the area. This was shortly after I had completed my mastery of earth magic, and I was starting my study of water. I found myself distracted far too often and decided to take a break, and at the same time, find some inspiration. So I traveled to the ocean to see what it was all about."

"Was it the most beautiful place you've seen?" Nera asked. "I'd love to see it myself."

"It was a lovely place to visit, yes," Seela replied. "But I much prefer the forest as my home."

"Tell them how you found me," Aqualia encouraged her.

"I was prowling about the ocean and stumbled across her on that little island."

"She was walking on the water's surface," Aqualia added. "I've lived my whole life on the sea and never seen anything like it. I thought I'd lost my mind."

"Well, I was partially sinking if truth be told," Seela stated. "She was far from shore, and I'd used quite a bit of magic to reach her. I was as surprised as she was that there was another soul upon the islet."

"What happened next?" Nera asked.

"I passed out," Aqualia replied, her voice full of humor.

"I used some magic to help her recover and remained at her side until she was fully healed," Seela said. "We passed the time talking and sharing stories until she was well enough to return home." Proudly, she added, "We've been friends ever since."

"Seela is a fascinating friend to have," Aqualia said, smiling.

"Aqualia's entire people are fascinating," Seela replied. "I was honored to be allowed as a guest in her waters. Her parents threw a banquet in my honor for helping their daughter." Shaking her head, she said, "My own family would never be so kind. They'd probably throw a party for someone bringing my dead carcass and placing it before them."

"Tell me about your family," Kwil implored her.

"There isn't much to tell, really," Seela replied. "My parents are deceased, and my only nearby relative is an uncle, who is also a master wizard. He owns the manor that was rightly mine by birth, but my being outcast meant that I would inherit nothing." There was a slight hint of bitterness in her tone, but a sigh of acceptance suggested she was over the disappointment.

"That isn't right," Nera commented.

"What's done is done," Seela replied, "and I have no desire to own the manor or live among those who would revile me. Still, I would like to have the medallion my mother wore. I played with it often as a child. She let me paw it while she would sing to me. My mother held great love for me, despite everyone else telling her I was a creature of evil. It pained her that I was sent away, but she had no power to stop it. She was a virtual prisoner to my father."

Nera nodded her understanding. She could easily relate to the way Seela's mother had been treated. It was all too common in Gatan society. "We have more in common than I realized," she said.

Kwil seemed lost in thought, as visions of his mother singing flooded his mind. Picturing Seela as a child in her mother's arms, he nearly wept at the sorrow of the two being forced to part. Silently, he vowed to retrieve this medallion for her. It was the least he could do for his mistress.

After dinner, Nera played her lute while Aqualia sang, her voice penetrating the souls of the listeners.

Walk with me upon the sand,
swim beside me 'neath the waves.
To the waters of eternity,
sleeping ever in our graves.

Hand in hand we drift to sleep,
our hearts entwined as one.
To the ever after
'neath the setting sun.

Enthralled by her voice, Kwil could barely move. He had fallen entirely under her spell, unable to resist her song. Nera gave him a knowing smile and patted his shoulder as she put her lute away.

"You have quite a talent for the lute," Aqualia said.

"Thank you," Nera replied. "Your voice is incredible."

"It is a gift," Aqualia said modestly.

With a yawn, Seela announced it was time for bed, and they made their way upstairs, each retiring to his or her own room. The Siren's song still echoing in their minds, they drifted off to sleep, images of the sea haunting their dreams.

Chapter 19

Over the next four days, Nera and Aqualia were inseparable. Aqualia had never been taught to play the lute, so she allowed Nera to give her a few lessons while she helped Nera refine her singing voice.

Curious about her new friend, Aqualia asked, "Why is it you don't study magic like your friend Kwil?"

"My father wanted me to be a master wizard, but it isn't the life I'd choose," she explained. "I spent a full year at the College before I escaped. I'm better off here where I can hear the music of the forest and practice any time I wish."

"I understand," the Siren replied. "A year, did you say?"

"Yes," Nera replied, wondering why it would interest her.

"Then you should have a magical store, correct?"

"I suppose I do," Nera replied. "It's probably very small, though."

"That's all you'll need," Aqualia replied, smiling. "Use it in your singing."

"What do you mean?" Nera asked.

"Just a touch of magic when you begin a song," she replied. "It will strengthen the music."

The thought had never occurred to Nera. She detested every moment at the College, and she never expected to use any of the magic she learned there. But Aqualia made a valid point. If she used it to augment her music, she could enhance her performance. Not by tricking her audience, but by enchanting the strings of her lute or, as the Siren suggested, add a touch of magic to her voice. "I think that's a fantastic idea," she replied, beaming. Kwil would be delighted to see her using magic. She decided not to tell him, and instead let him be surprised when next he heard her play.

"Since you are capable of magic, there is one spell I'd like to teach you," Aqualia said. "Don't worry, it isn't the kind of magic they would teach at the College. It's a bit of water magic, and my people use it often."

"Are you sure it's something I can learn?" she asked. After all, she was a Gatan, not a Siren.

"I'm certain you can," Aqualia replied. "Come with me."

Together they exited the cabin and took seats upon a fallen log. Despite the winter chill, there seemed to be hundreds of birds singing in the trees. Aqualia's presence had brought new magic to the Dark Forest.

"I want you to close your eyes and concentrate on the birdsong," the Siren said. "Block out every other thought and listen."

Nera did as she was bid. Several songs overlapped, high pitches, trills, descending notes, and every variation in between drew pictures in her mind. Multicolored feathers lingered in her vision as the music cut through all distractions. Even the wind whispered a low and melancholy tune.

At her side, Aqualia hummed softly to the forest. Then her song changed to a crystalline note, dangling on the winter wind. She held the note eight counts before allowing it to fall, switching to a flawless alto melody. The birds took notice and stood in revered silence until the Siren finished her song.

Nera opened her eyes to look upon her friend. "That was beautiful," she said, a tear in her eye.

"That, my friend, you must remember," Aqualia said. "I wish you to learn this melody, and use it with your magic. It will give you some power over nature, at least for a short time."

Nera was anxious to learn, never having heard magic crafted through music. This was something she could truly come to love. If there were more spells such as this, she might decide to continue her magical studies at some point.

After two hours practicing the Cry, Nera was able to produce the proper tones only a few times. Now she regretted not trying harder at the College. With greater stores, she would be able to perform the melody perfectly more often.

"It takes time to learn, and you will master it eventually," Aqualia said with an encouraging smile.

"Thank you for teaching me," Nera replied. Sadness crept into her heart as she knew her new friend would be leaving soon to return home. But Kwil would be interested in learning about the Cry, and the two could study at least that small amount of magic together. Maybe someday her path and Aqualia's would meet again.

* * * * *

Seela trotted down the stairs to meet Kwil for the day's lesson. He was already standing at attention, anticipating her arrival.

"Good morning," she said. "Today, we're going to perfect your skills at moving objects with magic."

"I already know how to do that," Kwil replied, a puzzled expression on his face. "You've seen me do it many times."

Frowning, Seela shook her head. "You can make things rise and fall and float around, but you might need to learn fine movements." Grabbing a piece of string from her desk drawer, she laid it in front of her student. "I want you to tie this in a knot using magic. And remember not to use words or finger movements."

Keeping his eyes open, Kwil focused on the string, visualizing it tying itself into a tight knot. The string began to twitch before lifting itself off the desk. As he concentrated on the magic, the string worked itself into a knot. Gently, he placed it back on the desk.

"I've done it," he said.

"Good work," Seela replied. "Now do that a hundred times."

Stumbling on his words, he managed to say, "But I did it on the first try." Why should he waste time doing it repeatedly if he had already mastered it?

"Yes, you did, and congratulations," she replied. "Now perfect it, and in the process, increase your stores a smidge." Slightly disappointed that her apprentice did not see the purpose of the lesson on his own, she sighed. Selecting a book from the shelf, she sat down to work on her own studies.

Kwil felt silly for questioning his mistress. There was a reason for every lesson, and he had missed it. She wanted him to learn delicate movements, allowing him to manipulate objects with fine detail. This could be useful in a multitude of situations, plus the boost to his magical stores from constant practice would be invaluable.

Setting his mind to the task, Kwil tied knots again and again until there was no string left to tie. "I've run out of string," he announced.

"You know how to fix that," Seela responded, not looking away from her reading.

Kwil felt redness creep into his face. Why did he speak without thinking? Of course he knew the spell to increase the length of the string. *Good job making yourself look stupid*, he thought. Hopefully soon he would fall into the role of a proper apprentice. Never question your master's orders, unless, of course, you're supposed to question them. The trick was knowing when to ask, and what question was the correct one. Learning magic was difficult, but getting to know the nuances of one's master was even harder.

For the next hour, Kwil tied knots in the string, adding length as needed to complete the task. When he finally finished, he said, "One hundred knots, Mistress. As you requested." He held the string out for her to observe.

"Well done," she replied. Next to the wall leaned a broom that was rarely used. Seela did most of her cleaning through magic, so it served a better purpose as a teaching aid. Retrieving it, she handed it to Kwil. "Choose one strand and remove it from the others. Pick a deep one."

Kwil stared at the tightly woven section of straw at the top of the broom, wondering how much force would be required to pull out a single strand. Focusing his mind to the middle of the straw, he tugged at a single strand, attempting to pull it away from the others. It held fast, so he closed his eyes and pictured it freeing itself from the confines of the other strands.

A small but audible snap sounded in his ears, startling him slightly, but he did not lose his concentration.

Seela watched with pride as the middle strand released itself and floated toward her student. "Excellent," she said. "You've proved that you can focus on a single object among many."

Immediately seeing the value in this lesson, Kwil asked, "Can I try again?" The most difficult aspect had been homing in on the particular strand he sought. Then it was just a matter of figuring out how much magic to use to move that one strand without harming the others. It was meticulous work, but he loved it.

"You may try again if you like, or we can move on to something else," she replied.

"Actually," he began, "could this same spell be used to separate mixtures? I'd love to learn more about potion making."

Seela's golden eyes lit up. "This spell would most definitely help in potion crafting, and I'd love to teach you more about it. You're learning is coming along quite nicely in other subjects, so I suppose it's about time to learn something different." Gracefully she hopped to the higher levels of the bookshelf, her paw tapping the spines of several tomes before she found the one she sought. Using magic, she sent the book Kwil's direction and laid it on the desk in front of him.

Before he could open the book, three more landed on top of it, followed soon after by a fourth. Seela dropped down to his side, another book floating softly after her.

"I suppose I should be giving you reading time every evening," she said. It had been decades since Rili left, and she'd had no student since. Her skills at planning lessons had fallen by the wayside. "There are far more spells than I can teach, and books are where you will learn the most about fire magic." She placed the fifth tome in front of him.

Staring at the deep red volume in front of him, he read the title: *Elemental Magic: Fire Volume One*. His eyes glistened as he beheld the prize in his hands. This was the start of his journey to master fire. The only disappointment was that it was the first volume. *I suppose I have to start at the beginning,* he decided, silently vowing to move to volume two within a week's time.

"Since I haven't mastered fire, you'll need to learn most of these spells on your own," she said. "Maybe when I'm ready you can teach me a thing or two."

Smiling at the prospect, he asked "Do I need to memorize the incantations if I won't be saying them?"

"A good question," she replied. "If you can visualize the spell, then no. But you should be familiar with the language. Otherwise you will have great difficulty in learning the things I cannot teach."

All of the books were written in ancient runes, so knowing the words would most certainly work in his favor. Even if he didn't speak them aloud, recognizing them would make learning easier. He couldn't help but wonder how many other wizards performed magic as Seela did, without incantations or gestures. "Are you part elf?" he asked, curious about her origins. There must be a reason she could perform magic in a non-Gatan fashion.

"No," she said, shaking her head. "I am a Feles. We have innate magical abilities as the elves do, but we do not inherit from their line. We have our ancestry in the Ancients."

"I'd like to know more about that," Kwil replied with interest.

"There are books about that too," she replied, pointing to a section on her shelf.

Kwil looked up at the tomes with wonder in his eyes. There were so many books here that he could keep himself busy for years. His only regret was that he couldn't read them all in a day.

Sensing his thoughts, Seela said, "If only I could inject the information into your mind." A gentle laugh escaped her lips. "It's hard to be patient when you're young, but trust me, the learning will come. You are far ahead of any other student your age. Keep reading and never stop. Until the day you leave this world, you will continue to read and learn."

Kwil began reading and didn't stop until late into the night. His eyelids grew far too heavy, and although he tried desperately to continue, his body would not allow it. His head nestled upon the aging pages, he fell fast asleep.

Early the next morning, Nera woke him with a gentle tap on his shoulder. "Aqualia is leaving," she said. "Come and say goodbye."

Regretting he hadn't spent more time with the Siren, Kwil followed Nera to the door. Aqualia smiled sweetly at him, noticing a smudge of ink upon his cheek, no doubt the result of his resting place for the night. He tried his best to avoid staring at her, but the pull she had on him was magnetic.

"It's been a pleasure," Aqualia said, hugging Seela goodbye.

"You're welcome back any time, my friend," Seela replied, tears in her golden eyes. It had been many years since their last visit, and only the wind knew for certain when they would meet again.

"Nera, you remember what I taught you," the Siren said. "Keep practicing, and most of all, believe in yourself."

"I will," Nera promised. She hugged the Siren tightly, sorry to see her go. In the last few days she had learned more than she ever imagined, not only about voice, but also about magic. She was eager to show Kwil her new skill.

"I'm sorry we didn't get to know each other better," Aqualia said to Kwil. "Perhaps on my next visit we can talk more."

"I'd like that," he replied. "Maybe when I'm ready to study water I could visit you and your people."

"An excellent idea," Aqualia said. "You should all come for a visit someday."

"You can count on it," Seela replied. She had not forgotten the warm welcome the Sirens had given her. They were far more accepting of her than her own kind, and she desired to swim among them once more. But not just yet. Now was the time to prepare Kwil for his future, and she had much yet she desired to learn. Perhaps after she mastered water magic she would visit Aqualia again, no matter how many years had passed.

"Farewell," the Siren said as she turned to leave. A few steps into the forest, she turned once to wave to her friends.

"Will she be safe in the forest?" Kwil asked, concerned.

"Aqualia can look out for herself," Seela replied. "She is a creature of magic, and her voice can bend others to her will. She will be quite safe."

Kwil regretted not learning more from the Siren. There was undoubtedly magic she could have taught him. Again he wished to learn everything at once. His patience was in short supply when it came to learning magic. If only there were a spell to plant all the knowledge in his mind at once. Failing that, he returned to his desk to continue his reading.

Nera watched wistfully as Aqualia disappeared into the distance. She closed the door and picked up her lute, strumming idly at the strings. Singing softly to herself, a flash of blue magic shone in her eyes.

Chapter 20

Eager to inform Kwil of the spell Aqualia had taught her, Nera approached him at his desk. Busy with his reading, he took no notice of her. She stood a moment wondering if he would look up, but his mind remained on his studies.

"Kwil," she said, excitement in her voice.

Startled, he looked up from his book. "What is it?" he asked.

"You're never going to believe what the Siren taught me," she said. "Such music as you've never heard."

"That's wonderful," he replied. "Will you play it for me?"

"I'll sing it," she said. Before she could vocalize the first note, Seela appeared in front of them, a wooden bucket clutched in her paw.

"I need water from the spring, Apprentice," she said, shoving the bucket toward Kwil. "Today you will have your first potions lesson, but I can't teach without fresh water."

Kwil gave Nera a regretful smile. He was looking forward to hearing her sing, but it would have to wait. Seela's commands took priority. As her apprentice, he must obey.

"Off you go," Seela said. "Nera, go with him. I don't want him lost out there." She winked a golden eye at the girl.

"It's only twenty yards behind the cabin," Kwil pointed out. "I'd have to be a complete idiot to get lost."

Nera chuckled softly. "The fresh air will do me good," she said.

Even on a short trip, Kwil enjoyed having Nera along. "Let's go, then," he said, grabbing hold of the bucket.

The pair stepped outside, the chill of winter immediately grabbing at their exposed skin. A menacing wind moaned its way through the trees, dark clouds overhead threatening to blanket the forest with snow.

"Let's hurry," Nera said, pulling her cloak around her. "It's freezing out here."

Walking at a brisk pace, they arrived at the spring. Its waters steamed as the warm spring water touched the cold air. Fire deep in the earth itself combined with this water, keeping it warm year-round. Its banks retained their green foliage, unlike the rest of the Dark Forest. Here there was life, while elsewhere all was cold and dormant.

Kneeling down, Kwil dipped the bucket into the water and brought it back out. "All done," he announced. It was a quick venture out of doors, but a necessary one. Standing up, he swiveled on a heel, preparing to return to the cabin. Nera's expression, however, gave him pause. She stared wide-eyed at something on the far bank, her mouth slightly open. Kwil could sense her fear as her muscles tightened and her breath became barely audible. Slowly lifting a finger, she pointed to the source of her fear.

Cautiously Kwil turned, observing only from the corner of his eye. A massive figure stood unmoving on the opposite bank, a large object clutched in its hand. Positioning himself for a better look, Kwil moved at a snail's pace. If he moved too quickly, whoever it was might consider him a threat. Keeping calm was his best chance to avoid a confrontation.

Stunned by what his eyes beheld, Kwil stood with his feet rooted to the spot. On the far bank stood an ogre, its thick gray skin ornamented with warts. In one hand it held a wooden cudgel, which dragged lazily against the ground. The creature narrowed its eyes to get a better look at the two people before it. Raising its cudgel, it scratched the back of its neck.

Kwil took two steps backward, and Nera stepped sideways to join him. Neither had encountered an ogre before, but both expected the worst. Any armed creature would give them pause, but one as massive as this ogre meant serious trouble.

"Should we run?" Nera asked. Seela had most likely dealt with ogres before if they lived among these woods. She would know how to deal with him.

Before Kwil could reply, the ogre lifted the cudgel over his head and belched out a deep roar. In two strides it crossed the stream, its eyes focused on the apprentice.

Dropping his bucket, Kwil dodged to one side while Nera went the opposite direction. The ogre's foot crashed against the spot where the pair had stood.

It turned its focus to Kwil, ignoring the Gatan for the time being.

Kwil's magical instincts kicked in, and he prepared a fire spell to toss at the beast. It was approaching too fast, forcing him to jump out of the way to avoid a blow from the cudgel. Hiding himself behind a tree, he focused his mind to fire, summoning a red blaze in his hand. Hurling it toward the ogre, he watched in shock as it bounced from the ogre's thick skin without fazing it.

Nera jumped from behind, grabbing tightly onto the ogre's arm. With a look of confusion, the ogre stared at the furred creature clinging onto his arm. She attempted to bite through his skin, but it was too tough for her to penetrate. The ogre shook its arm, forcing Nera to relax her grip. Landing on the ground, she rolled out of the way as the cudgel slammed down next to her.

Frantically, Kwil searched his mind for a different fire spell that might break through the ogre's defenses. As if a light went on, he remembered the spell Seela first taught him to weaken his enemies. He needed to drain the creature's magic in order to subdue it. Conjuring a beam of light, he focused it at the ogre, holding it firmly in his power. Drawing power away from it, he soon realized that the ogre had only a tiny store of magic.

Enraged by the violation, the ogre closed in on Kwil. Its heavy foot landed next to him, the young mage standing only to the height of the ogre's knee. As the ogre lifted its cudgel to smash him to bits, Kwil threw a fire spell at the weapon, setting it ablaze. Feeling the heat next to his face, the ogre dropped the cudgel. Kwil rolled away, hoping to avoid the falling object.

Roaring in anger, the ogre watched as its weapon burned to ash. Ripping at a limb, it tore it away from the tree and swung it in Kwil's direction. The wizard reacted with a burst of energy, forcing the limb away and knocking the ogre slightly off-balance. It managed to steady itself quickly and stepped forward to pummel the mage.

Knowing he couldn't move fast enough to avoid the beast's attack, Kwil used the energy blast to move himself from harm's way. The ogre roared its displeasure, the ground shaking under the weight of its stamping feet. Without hesitation, Kwil returned to the spell to absorb the creature's magic. Its stores were dry, but Kwil had another idea. The same magic could be used to weaken the beast further, draining his energy to the point of exhaustion. If only Kwil could hold the spell long enough, he would have the creature under his control. But the ogre was advancing, and Kwil knew he would have to move away, breaking his concentration and his spell.

Not knowing how else to save her friend, Nera thought of the magic Aqualia had taught her. The song swam in her mind, its notes intertwining with her soul. Opening her mouth, a single note released itself, thin at first but becoming more intense as she held it. The ogre dropped its tree limb and placed his hands over his ears, shaking his head from side to side.

Kwil watched in amazement as the ogre groaned and staggered sideways. Only yards away, Nera stood, her voice cutting through the winter air. It was her, he realized, that had the creature under her power. Somehow she had produced magic through her voice, and she had stopped the ogre in its tracks.

"Enough!" a voice called, silencing Nera. It was Seela, who had emerged from her cabin to remedy the situation. "Impressive," she said as she passed Nera.

Approaching the ogre, she extended a bundle toward him. He dropped his hands from his ears and looked curiously at the Feles. Taking the bundle, he peered inside it before nodding his approval.

"Your help is most appreciated," Seela said.

With a soft grunt, the ogre marched off into the trees, disappearing from sight.

Scrambling to his feet, Kwil asked, "What was that all about?"

"He is a friend of mine," Seela explained. "I asked him to test the two of you, particularly Nera." Looking at Kwil, she said, "Your abilities are coming along nicely too. You are becoming wiser at choosing your spells, but you still need work."

"Then this was a trick?" he asked.

"There are few real-world opportunities to test you," Seela replied. "Don't worry. I was watching the entire time and would have intervened had you needed me." After a pause, she added, "The ogre meant neither of you any harm, but I asked him to be as forceful as possible."

"We could have been killed," Nera said, still in shock.

"I wouldn't have let that happen," Seela assured her. "Aqualia would be pleased with your mastery of the Cry."

Nera swallowed hard. It had taken little effort on her part, yet she had managed to subdue the massive creature. "I didn't realize how powerful the spell was," she said.

"The Cry can be used only every few days, and it will work only on certain creatures of low intelligence," Seela explained. "The effect does not last long, but if you work hard at it, you might be able to control people as Aqualia is able to do."

Nera didn't know if she'd ever have the powers of a Siren, nor did she desire to control other people. But the desire to learn more about this spell and other spells based in music was growing inside her. This was the magic she desired, but she did not know it until recently. The magic she was taught at the College could never compare with this.

"Aqualia taught you magic?" Kwil asked, amazed. "You were incredible. I've never read about any spell like that."

Nera smiled shyly, unsure how to reply. Pride radiated from her friend as he praised her magical ability.

"I can't believe you learned that in only a few days." he remarked.

"What's so special about that?" she asked. "You learn spells in hours, sometimes minutes."

"Yes, but I have the desire," he replied. "You've always resisted learning magic. Now you're mastering a form of magic I never knew existed." His heart swelled with pride as he looked upon his friend. "Maybe you can teach me how to do that."

Seela shook her head. "The Cry can be taught only by the Sirens. You'll have to wait until Aqualia returns or you go to visit her."

"Is there no way to learn music magic without Aqualia?" Nera asked, hoping that wasn't the case.

"I have some books that explain other spells," she replied. "Only the Cry is exclusive to the Sirens. There is much you can learn here."

"I'd like to learn it too," Kwil replied. "But I'm afraid I'm not much of a singer, and I can't play an instrument."

"You could learn," Nera said.

"And perhaps one day he shall," Seela interjected. "For now he is learning elemental magic, and he is mastering fire. I know you youngsters want to know everything right away, but it isn't possible. One must learn these things in steps."

"Can you teach me to master music magic?" Nera asked, hopeful.

"I cannot," Seela replied. "But that won't prevent you from mastering it on your own. Not all magic is learned in the same way. The music is within you, and if you study hard, you will work great feats of magic. The path you choose to take with that is up to you."

"I don't understand," Nera said. Kwil had a destiny ahead of him. According to Seela, he was the one who would free the humans of Gi'gata. She fully intended to help him with that, but the fondest desire of her heart was to make beautiful music and share it with the world.

"You may use it to perform magic as Kwil and I do," Seela replied. "Or you may use it to compose works of music and perfect your skills with various musical instruments."

"Now I think I understand," she said with a smile. The choices before her were broad, as broad as those that Kwil would be given. Her form of magic was something entirely different, one that she would have to learn on her own. No school could teach her, only her heart could do that. The magic needed only to be pulled from within her.

To Kwil, Seela said, "I still need that water if we're going to learn potions today."

"Of course, Mistress," he replied, rushing to collect the bucket. Refilling it with water, he returned with the others to the cabin.

Seela immediately went to the shelf to retrieve a few books for Nera. "These are a good place to start," she said. "Learn these things and use them in your music. You'll figure things out soon enough."

Nera was happy to comply. She had never been one for reading, but reading about music and the magic she could make with it would not feel like a chore. This was something her heart truly desired. Snuggling up next to the fire, she opened one of the books and thumbed through the pages.

"The potion I'm going to teach you to make is a simple one," Seela said to Kwil. "It will do nicely for your first lesson."

"What does the potion do?" he asked.

"It will help you maintain focus when you cast a spell," Seela replied.

"Like when the ogre attacked, and I had to drop the spell to run," Kwil replied. His mind could not hold the spell when he had to concentrate on fleeing.

"Exactly," she said. "This is something that comes with practice. In time, you will be able to cast spells while moving without losing your focus. It's a matter of discipline. For now, the potion will help."

"How long will it take to train my mind?" he wondered.

Sighing, Seela replied, "You are an impatient young man." She shook her head. "In time you will cast two or even three spells at once. You will not need to look at your opponent to strike him, and you will be able to hold a spell despite interruptions." She squeezed his hand. "You must learn patience, though. This is not an easy task, and you need practice. Your thirst for knowledge is insatiable. I have no doubt you will master this quicker than most."

Seela's words of encouragement pleased him. If she had faith in him, then he would too. All he needed was time.

Chapter 21

As the months passed, winter's chill gave way to a fine spring, followed by the heat of summer. Kwil had spent every waking moment studying and unlocking the secrets of the forest with Seela as his guide. From her library, he had read hundreds of books cover to cover, memorizing every spell he could find. New techniques presented themselves, and he made every effort to incorporate them into his training. He was forming his own brand of magic, one that combined techniques of humans, elves, and Gatans. Though he had focused his efforts to mastering fire, he could perform spells from all the schools, thanks to Seela's guidance.

Seela was beyond pleased with her apprentice's accomplishments. He was a quick learner, and his eagerness had not diminished since day one. She doubted any other student outside of elven lands could learn so quickly. Not only was he talented, he was dedicated. He never took a break, always insisting on finishing one more book before going to bed at night.

Today, Seela planned to test Kwil on his most challenging spell yet. He had learned it in steps, and now it was time to put together what he had learned to see how quickly he could master it. The sorceress had high hopes for him. The test would be challenging, but she anticipated he would succeed.

Kwil trotted down the stairs at sunup, ready to show his mistress what he could do. He had an inkling what the test would be, and he felt mostly prepared. His only wish would be to master it on the first try, but that was unlikely. Reminding himself that it was the mastery of the spell that mattered, not how long it took, he presented himself before his mistress.

"Ah, there you are," Seela said. "Let's begin." Circling around him, she observed his posture and breathing. He appeared bright and healthy, perfectly suited to the task she was about to give him. "These past few months, you have mastered simple changes to your form." Under her tutelage, he had learned to change his eye and hair color, as well as his height and build. Now, she was about to present him with his ultimate challenge. "Today I want to see you present yourself as a Gatan."

Kwil could hardly breathe. He could hide himself against any background, and he could alter the details of his looks, but he had never changed himself into an entirely different form. How was this even possible? Could Seela present herself as a human? Kwil had never seen her do that. She could easily change her size, and likely her coloration, but could she hide her identity as a Feles? Or was she asking him to do the impossible?

Nera descended the stairs in time to hear Seela's request. Carefully stepping across the room, her feet made no sound against the floor. This was not the time to break her friend's concentration, but she had to see him perform this spell. Silently she took a seat, her hands pressed close to her heart.

Taking in a deep breath, Kwil wondered if he should question his mistress. Did she truly expect him to do this, or was he supposed to admit that it couldn't be done? Beads of sweat developed on his forehead as he weighed his options. *I can do this,* he decided.

Everything she has taught me has brought me to this point. I will not fail.

Seela's eyes gleamed as she watched the change in Kwil's expression. She knew he had found his confidence. Now all he had to do was visualize the magic and let it flow.

Focusing his mind to the spell, Kwil pictured himself in Gatan form. Patches of gray fur erupted from his skin, his concentration faltering. The sensation was not pleasant. It was slightly itchy and had an unnatural heaviness.

"Keep trying," Seela encouraged him.

Trying again, he managed somewhat better results. Most of his skin was covered in gray fur, but several bald patches gave him a disheveled appearance. His eyes narrowed, his pupils changed to slits, and his ears migrated to the top of his head, standing at attention. The slightest sound caused them to rotate, searching for the source of the noise. Intrigued, Kwil pushed harder, closing his eyes to block out the world. A tail sprouted from his backside, extending to half his body length.

Opening his eyes, he ran his hand over his arm, stroking the soft fur. His sense of smell was heightened, his whiskers twitching slightly. "This is amazing," he said. Not only had his appearance changed, but his abilities had as well. He had the hearing, sight, and sense of smell that came along with being Gatan, his human senses paling in comparison.

Nera cupped her hands over her mouth, stifling a laugh. Kwil's tail was twitching back and forth at a rapid pace. It stopped briefly, wrapping itself around his leg.

Feeling the compression, Kwil looked down at his leg. He tried to move the tail, but it would not obey. Using his hands, he tried to pry it away, but he could not. "What do I do?" he asked.

Seela couldn't contain her laughter. "It's your tail," she said. "You must make it obey you."

Visualizing the tail in a resting position, Kwil hoped to force it to behave. Instead, it stuck straight out like the branch of a tree. Frustrated, he decided to leave the tail as it was and focus on the bald patches instead. One by one, he corrected the flaws in his pelt and admired his reflection in Seela's mirror.

As his focus shifted elsewhere, the tail went limp behind him. When he tried to raise or lower it, it simply laid flat, ignoring him. "How does this work?" he asked, his eyes pleading with Nera.

"It's like moving your arm or leg," she replied. Never having used magic on her own tail, she did not know what other advice to give. "Treat it like any other body part."

Remembering the delicate finger movements of Gatan magic, Kwil realized his tail might work in the same way. Though he wasn't allowed to use his fingers to cast spells, he might be able to focus his magic to the tail as he once had his fingers. Channeling his magic through the tail, it quickly snapped to attention. He swished it left, then right, then formed a tight circle. Taking a few steps, he lifted the end slightly off the ground to avoid dragging it. "I think I'm getting the hang of it," he announced, a crooked smile on his lips.

Moving next to Nera, he wrapped his tail around hers, as if they were shaking hands. Nera laughed, followed soon after by Kwil.

"You make an interesting Gatan," she said.

"He does indeed," Seela stated. "You must keep working on this spell and perfect it. This is the spell that will allow you to walk among Gatans unhindered. You will be seen as one of them, not a mere slave. This is how you will do your finest work."

Kwil understood. This was the spell that would allow him to free the slaves of Gi'gata, and it was probably the most useful one he could learn. No longer would he have to live in fear. He would not be falsely accused, nor would he be punished without a trial. He could even practice magic freely, without anyone calling for his execution. Seela had taught him a most powerful spell, and he must put it to good use.

"I will keep practicing until I drop, Mistress," he promised her.

"I don't doubt that you will," she replied. "I expect you'll have it perfected in a day or two." Her gold eyes conveyed a hint of sadness. Kwil had learned so quickly, and their time together might soon be coming to an end. He was a fine student, but he would not remain a student forever.

"Mistress?" Kwil asked as he continued to practice. "Are you able to change your form to a human?"

"No, I can't," she replied. "I am a Feles, and I cannot change into any humanoid form. It is forbidden me, but if I chose to, I could change into any beast creature that exists."

He thought about it for a moment and said, "That still doesn't seem fair." Why should she have any restrictions on her magic?

"I have been given many gifts of magic already," she replied. "I have the lifespan of the Ancients as well as their talents for magic. Believe me, I am not hindered by the lack of humanoid features. Now come. There is someone I'd like you to meet."

Seela led Kwil and Nera through the forest, the summer's warmth bringing various shades of green to the Dark Forest. With the trees fully leaved, there was even less light reaching the forest floor, but the feeling was less ominous than in winter.

Only a few miles away, they spotted a dark figure moving in the distance. Seela approached the figure without reservation. Kwil and Nera stuck close by her, anxious to meet whatever it was. As it came into view, they could see the outline of a horse. It was covered in sleek black hair, its mane and tail flowing gently on the breeze. When its gaze fell upon them, both were taken in by its gleaming orange eyes.

Unnerved, Nera wished to go no farther. "What manner of creature is that?" she asked.

"He is a puca," Seela replied. "And he's no stranger than I." She could sense Nera's uneasiness, but there was no need for it. "Come and meet him," she said. "He won't harm you, especially with me around."

Reluctantly Nera followed, trusting in Seela and Kwil's magic. The puca stared straight at her, his eyes seeming to penetrate her soul. Her better judgment told her to avoid such a creature, but her curiosity grew with each step.

"This is Dirnda," Seela said, her paw raised toward the creature. The pair touched noses, the puca lowering himself to meet the Feles. "He is my friend." She gestured for Kwil and Nera to come forward.

The puca focused his sights on Nera, stepping forward to greet her. Summoning her courage, she placed a hand gently on his nose. Sensing the nervousness in his guest, the puca reduced his size, changing to the form of a brown-furred rabbit. Nera's apprehensions melted away, a smile spreading across her face.

Kwil knelt next to the rabbit, examining him for any sign of his previous form. "Incredible," he said. "Does he use the same method as we do?"

"The puca uses a similar technique," Seela replied, "but his power is limitless. He is a creature of the earth, and as long as he is in contact with earth, his magic remains strong."

"Fascinating," Kwil replied, still staring at the rabbit. As he watched, the rabbit changed form again, this time becoming humanoid. His green-gray skin and long nose reminded Kwil of the goblins he had seen in his reading. Taken aback, he returned to his feet and stepped away.

"Don't worry," Seela said. "Dirnda is a friend. He will not harm you. He is not the evil goblins you've heard of. This is merely one of his many forms."

A deep throaty laugh, escaped the goblin's lips, his manner full of mischief. Taking two strides toward Kwil, he extended his hand in friendship. Kwil took the puca's hand, only to be pulled off his feet, landing heavily in the dirt. Dirnda cackled wildly with laughter, his hands leaning against his knees as he doubled over with glee.

"Why did you do that? Nera demanded, helping the mage from the ground.

Dirnda made no reply. Instead, he changed to the form of a goat and charged toward the girl. His head connected with her midsection, sending her backward, stumbling. She landed on her backside, a lump of anger rising in her throat.

Seela raised a paw to stop Nera from attacking. "All right, Dirnda, that's enough," she said. "We have no time for play."

"Then why bring them here?" Dirnda asked, returning to his goblin form. His mischievous voice was full of disappointment. Clearly he wanted to amuse himself at the expense of his visitors.

"I wanted them to meet you so the three of you might become friends," Seela explained.

"I see," Dirnda replied with a laugh. For a second time he approached Kwil, his hand extended. "Friends," he said.

Kwil glanced at Seela, who gave a slight nod. Reaching out, he took the puca's hand. Dirnda gave the mage's hand two good shakes before releasing it. He tipped his cloth hat in Nera's direction. Nera crossed her arms and pursed her lips.

Deciding that the puca was a friend, Kwil asked, "Can you teach me how to shift into different creatures as you do?"

Dirnda chuckled and shook his head. "I'm no teacher," he said. "But if you can learn by watching, you're welcome to try." His body contorted as he shifted back into the form of a black horse. Rearing up onto his hind legs, he gave a loud whinny, his front hooves hammering the ground.

Impressed, Kwil asked Seela, "Can I become something that large?"

"There are no limits," she replied, "but you will need more practice than you have the patience for."

Kwil watched as Dirnda galloped in a circle, his stride matching that of the creature whose form he had taken. "Does he have the strength and stamina of a true horse when he's in that form, or is it just an illusion?" Seela was definitely stronger in her panther form, but the puca was so strange to him, he couldn't be sure.

"Climb aboard and find out," Dirnda called to the young man.

Nera stepped forward to stop him, but a glance from Seela halted her. Kwil eagerly approached the puca, who knelt and allowed him to climb onto his back. Nera stood at Seela's side, her breathing shallow and heart rate rising.

"No need to worry," Seela reassured her.

Dirnda sprung forward, the mage grasping desperately at the horse's mane. The two bolted out of sight, the echo of Dirnda's hooves bouncing from tree to tree.

"He's going to fall off," Nera commented, clenching her jaw. This was a bad idea.

"Nonsense," Seela replied. "He's smart enough to use magic to prevent himself from falling."

In the distance, Kwil was indeed using magic to hold himself on the horse. Dirnda raced through the forest, zigzagging through the trees and bounding over fallen branches. His muscles rippled beneath his sleek black coat, proving he had truly acquired the power of the animal he appeared to be. Amazed by the magic that had created it, Kwil was overjoyed. This was the magic he craved, and here was a creature born to it.

Returning to the others, Kwil hopped down from Dirnda's back, visibly out of breath. "Amazing," he managed to say. He could see Nera was still upset, so he laid a reassuring hand on her shoulder. She smiled in spite of herself, glad to see that her friend had returned unharmed. She could not stay angry when there was no need.

Laughing, Dirnda said, "Thank you for introducing us, Seela. The boy is quite amusing. Feel free to visit any time." He glanced at Nera and flashed a toothy smile before galloping away.

Seela waved a paw in goodbye. "It's getting late," she said. "We should get back."

Still reeling from his wild ride through the forest, Kwil was all smiles as they walked back to the cabin. Bubbling with energy, he continued his practice late into the night, not stopping until he was completely void of magic. Collapsing onto his bed, he dreamed of magic in various forms, watching spellbound as it shifted and swirled before him. The stars themselves twisted and swayed, dancing to the magic of the forest.

Chapter 22

After a week of practicing around the clock, Kwil perfected his shape-shifting spell. He could now transform himself into a Gatan at a moment's notice, and hold the spell for several hours. No more bare patches or uncontrollable tail twitches.

"All right then, let's see it," Seela said, crossing her paws.

Kwil gave a glance at Nera, who was watching over the top of her book. All of his practice had been done in private, and she was anxious to see her friend's new look.

Visualizing himself as a Gatan, Kwil immediately began to change. On top of his skin, silver-gray fur erupted, covering his body in a shining pelt. Dark stripes added themselves over the gray, giving him a more distinguished look. His eyes became yellow, and his whiskers grew long. A slender tail protruded from his backside, laying gently at rest under his command.

"Bravo!" Seela cried, beaming with pride.

Nera jumped from her seat, her hands clutched over her mouth.

"What do you think?" Kwil asked her.

"You're actually kind of handsome," she replied.

"I'm not handsome when I'm human?" he asked, feigning insult.

"Well, not really," she replied honestly. "You're kind of pink and hairless."

Kwil laughed, unfazed by her remark.

Seela placed her paws on each side of Kwil's face. "You look marvelous," she said. "Simply marvelous." With a sigh, she added, "It amazes me how far you've come since your arrival." The statement was true. Ever since he arrived, he'd hardly stopped studying and practicing for a minute. Over the past few months, he had blossomed into a fine sorcerer, one capable of as much or more than any graduate of the College. Seela suspected he was far more dedicated than most of those students. Like Nera, many of them had not enrolled by choice. Kwil's love of magic and innate abilities gave him an edge over the others. Whether it took a day or a year, he would master any spell she offered him. "You haven't been neglecting your fire practice have you?" she asked, cocking her head to the side. After all, he intended to master the element. It wouldn't do to let his practice slip.

"Not at all," he responded. With a blink of his eyes, he transformed his fur to orange, appearing as if he were glowing with fire. Heat radiated from his pelt, his eyes flashing red. Turning up his palms, fire appeared in each hand, rising to the height of his chin. He allowed the flames to dance and sputter before releasing them, launching them high into the air and snuffing them before they reached the floor.

Nera clapped her hands, impressed by the sudden change. She had witnessed his practice with fire magic, and she knew he could be quite dangerous when he wanted to. Luckily, he was only putting on a show for now.

Seela did not reply, so Kwil performed another spell. Glancing around the cabin, he located every candle present. Without moving a muscle, he lit them simultaneously, including the ones upstairs.

Seela's stoic expression gave way to a crooked grin. "Well done," she said. "Now put them out before you burn down my cabin."

Kwil obeyed, snuffing out the candles all at once. Changing back to his human form, he looked upon his master. "Would you say I've earned a day or two off?" he asked, grinning.

The question came as a surprise to Seela. Kwil had never even expressed an interest in taking a break. "I don't see why not," she replied after a slight pause. "But what are you planning to do if you're not studying?"

"I'd like to explore the forest," he replied. "Get to know the surroundings and any creatures that might be around," he added. "I'm hoping Nera will join me."

Nera looked at him with surprise. He was usually content to have his nose stuck in a book. Yearning for adventure wasn't exactly in his character.

"Will you come along?" he asked.

Nodding, she replied, "Of course I will."

"I suppose you can take care of yourselves," Seela said. "You've certainly earned a day or two off, but don't stay away too long. Make sure you're practicing as well. I wouldn't want you to become rusty." Pleased that her student was ready to explore the surroundings, she began planning in her mind what to do with her time without him. A long soak in the tub sounded like a good start.

"We won't be gone more than two days," he promised.

Nera caught sight of a sparkle in his eye, one that spoke of secrets. Kwil was planning something, and she couldn't guess what it was. It was clear he didn't want Seela to know about it, but Nera was determined to find out.

Seela trotted off upstairs while Kwil collected some food items for the trip. He didn't hear Nera approaching from behind.

"All right," she said. "Seela's gone upstairs, so tell me what you're planning. What's this trip really about?"

Kwil glanced around the room before retrieving a bit of parchment from his pocket. "This," he said, passing it to her.

Unfolding the parchment, Nera asked, "What is this place?" A location was marked on the map, obviously the destination Kwil had in mind.

"It's Seela's childhood home," Kwil replied. "I want to retrieve the medallion she spoke of."

Nera remembered Seela's story and the medallion she had been forced to leave behind. "It's sweet of you, Kwil, but how are you going to convince her uncle to give it to you?"

"I don't plan to ask," he replied, grinning. These months of learning had given him new confidence. Master wizard or not, he was ready to face any obstacle to retrieve this treasure for Seela. She had given him his dream, and he would give her this gift in gratitude.

"This is dangerous, Kwil," Nera said, unsure whether she wanted to go along with him. "Humans can't just go barging into a noble lord's manor. You could be killed."

"I don't plan to go as a human," he replied. "No one's going to suspect me."

"This is insane," she commented. "Are you sure you can do this?"

"Nera, I've never been more confident of anything in my life," he said sincerely. "I'm ready to do this. Please come with me." He had not forgotten Seela's words. Nera's friendship was essential if he was to achieve his destiny. Without her, he might not succeed.

"Of course I will," she replied. How could she refuse? He might get into trouble, and who else would be there to help him? He was her dearest friend, and if he felt himself ready to face this man, she would help in any way she could.

"Master Arsden's manor is only a two-day walk from here," Kwil began. "But we can get there much faster if Dirnda will help us."

"Wait a minute," Nera said, recognizing the name. "Seela's uncle is Master Arsden?"

"Yes," Kwil replied. "Do you know him?"

"I know of him," Nera said. "He's a slave breeder. A wealthy one. There will be guards everywhere." Not only did he need guards to keep the slaves in line, he needed them to avoid theft. Bands of thieves had been known to steal slaves by the dozen and take them to smaller markets throughout the land. That way they avoided regulations and questions.

"Then we'll just have to be extra careful," Kwil decided. Even if the place was secure, he would find a way in.

"I hope you know what you're doing," Nera said. Slinging her bag over her shoulder, she led the way out the door and into the forest.

Side by side, the two headed to the same location where they had first met Dirnda. Summer's heat penetrated the dense forest, and the humidity had risen to an uncomfortable level. Kwil wondered how long it would take a master of air magic to alter the weather, but since Seela had never made such an offer, he decided it must be incredibly difficult. Or perhaps it took a team of wizards like the island elves he had read about. His thoughts turned to visiting them someday, maybe even finding his long-lost elven relatives.

A loud whistle from Nera brought him out of his reverie. She had paused a few steps ahead of him and seen no trace of the puca. But Dirnda hadn't gone far. Hearing the whistle, he galloped into sight, appearing from deep within the forest.

With a toss of his long, black mane, Dirnda said, "It's good to see you both again. What brings you to this part of the forest?"

"I would ask a favor of you," Kwil replied, hopeful the puca would be willing to listen.

"Favor?" Dirnda echoed. "I owe you no such thing."

"I know that," Kwil said, "but I need your help. Will you at least hear me out?"

The puca thought a moment, his orange eyes staring through the young mage. "Very well," he eventually replied.

"We wish to retrieve a medallion for Mistress Seela," Kwil explained. "If you could give us a ride to her family home, we would be in your debt."

Nera's eyes shifted nervously. She wasn't sure she wanted the puca's help. A creature given to tricks, she wasn't sure he could be trusted long enough to be of assistance. He might gallop off, leaving them at the side of the road merely because he thought it would be funny.

After a moment's consideration, Dirnda said, "I will do this, but you must promise to do something for me in return."

"What do you need?" Kwil asked. Whatever the puca needed, Kwil would do it.

"I don't need anything right now," Dirnda replied. "I'll name the favor later, and you must come through for me, no matter what."

"Agreed," Kwil replied without hesitation.

Nera sighed and looked at the ground. She didn't like the idea of agreeing to perform some unknown task. There was no way of knowing what the puca would ask for. "I don't think that's wise," she whispered to Kwil.

"It's the only way," he replied. "If we're gone too long, Seela might worry and come looking for us. And riding there will save energy that we might need." He was well aware that he might have to fight his way in, and he intended to arrive at full strength.

"I just hope you aren't getting in over your head," she muttered.

Kwil climbed onto Dirnda's back and reached a hand down to assist Nera. She took a seat behind him, her arms wrapped tightly around his waist. Laying a hand on Dirnda's neck, Kwil transmitted the location of the manor, the image of the map moving from one mind to the other.

The puca lunged forward, speeding through the forest, sending dirt and strands of grass flying in his wake. Nera pressed her face against Kwil's back and squeezed her eyes shut. The puca maneuvered dangerously close to the trees, adjusting course without losing speed. Paying no heed to the comfort of the riders, he galloped on, his thoughts fixated on his destination.

Exhilarated by the puca's speed, Kwil watched as the twisted trees of the Dark Forest thinned, becoming a brighter, more inviting section of woods. The miles passed by, and in two hours' time, they had cleared the forest altogether. Trees grew sparsely in this area, meadows and open spaces instead appearing before his eyes.

Though the puca did not slow, the ride became smoother as they entered the fields. Nera dared to open her eyes, looking upon pastures of green as they sped by. Sheep and cattle came in and out of view, fading to tiny dots on the horizon. The air was crisp and clean, the sun bright overhead as they flew across the countryside, never slowing.

Nera's heart pounded in her chest, her hands still firmly clasped around her friend. As they reached the road, Dirnda made a hard left, turning away from the heavily traveled path in favor of the green pastures. Nera felt herself slipping, nearly coming off the side of the steed. Kwil felt the tug at his waist and cast white magic over his friend, willing her to stay put. Feeling the magic's pull, she whispered a quick thanks in his ear, but the pounding of the puca's hooves prevented the mage from hearing it.

The lack of obstacles allowed Dirnda to increase his speed, his hooves nearly flying over the soft earth. The landscape changed from scenic to a blur, forcing them to close their eyes to ward off dizziness. Kwil turned his attention to his magic, practically gluing Nera and himself to the stallion's back.

Dirnda pressed on without a care, loving every minute of the race. Running was his freedom—the time when he was most alive.

Shortly before sunset, the trio arrived within sight of Master Arsden's manor. Nestled safely behind a tall iron fence, the compound stretched out before them. It was easily three times the size of the Orva manor, and Kwil realized that it might take longer than expected to locate the medallion. It could be anywhere within the manor, and if Arsden would not give up the information, Kwil might be in for a long search. He searched his mind for a spell that would help him locate it, but could not recall anything useful. Without knowing what the medallion looked like, he wondered how he would be able to visualize it and connect with it through magic. He kept these worries to himself, not wanting to trouble Nera or give her cause to insist they return home. He would simply have to find a way.

Relieved that the ride was over, Nera dismounted and resisted the urge to kiss the ground. It had certainly shaved hours off their travel, but she would have preferred a slower pace. She was not looking forward to the return journey.

"Will you wait for us?" Kwil asked the puca.

"I don't have all night," Dirnda replied. "How long will this take?" He pawed at the ground, anxious to continue moving.

"I'm not sure," Kwil replied. "But we might need to get away quickly. I'm not sure we can do it without you."

Dirnda grunted and stamped the ground. "Fine," he said. "I will try to stay in the area."

"Thanks," Kwil said. It wasn't the firmest of promises, but he would take it.

Nera watched as Dirnda circled and trotted away from the manor. "What now?" she asked. "How do we get inside?"

Observing the black iron gate, Kwil said, "We go through the gate."

"Won't we get caught?" she asked, raising an eyebrow.

In an instant, Kwil transformed into his Gatan form, his silver fur gleaming in the fading light. "We can pretend we've come to buy a slave," he replied.

Nera shook her head. "You don't buy directly from breeders," she said. "Breeders send the slaves to markets. They don't sell from their homes."

Kwil's shoulders fell slightly as he realized his plan to get inside wouldn't work. In all his studies, he hadn't bothered to learn the details of Gi'gata's slave trade. Looking at the fence, he counted three separate locks.

Apparently Arsden didn't welcome visitors. "We'll just have to break in," he said.

"Climb the fence?" she asked, looking at the rails.

Kwil placed a hand on the metal and felt a tingling sensation. "It has a magical charge," he said. "We don't want to be in contact with it for long." Climbing the fence was out. He would have to hold onto the metal too long.

"Can you break the spell?" she asked.

"Not without alerting the person who placed the enchantment," he replied. "The only option is to open this gate and walk through without being seen."

"And that's most likely impossible," Nera said, crossing her arms. It seemed the mission had failed before it had begun.

"We're getting inside," Kwil said, his eyes flashing red. "Even if it means blowing this gate to pieces."

Chapter 23

"Don't get carried away," Nera cautioned. "You can't start tossing fireballs at the gate, or all the guards are going to come running." She looked the gate up and down before placing her hand on one of the locks. "Why don't you try unlocking these first?"

The fire dwindled from Kwil's eyes as he realized the wisdom of Nera's suggestion. There was still a chance of getting inside quietly. Chiding himself for not thinking rationally, he stepped forward to examine the lock. Through his magic, he viewed the mechanism inside the metal casing and counted four separate tumblers. They were in good repair and would not easily open without the key, but Kwil had to try.

In his mind, Kwil focused on the first tumbler, avoiding all contact with the other three. Gently he manipulated the pins, forcing the spring to compress and the other components to move into the correct alignment. Breathing out, he turned to Nera. "One down," he said. Blocking out all other thoughts, he turned his mind to the next three tumblers, positioning them in half the time of the first.

Kwil handed the open lock to Nera, who tossed it casually to the ground. There wouldn't be a need to relock the gate while they were leaving. "Two more to go," she said.

As he stared inside the second lock, Kwil could see that it had rusted over time. The mechanisms did not move easily, and he suspected opening it would prove difficult, even with the key. Using the heat from his body, he attempted to melt the rust away from the metal, allowing the springs to glide freely. He did not achieve the intended result, however. Instead of melting the rust, he softened the entire lock along with its chain. It fused to the gate as it cooled.

"I hope you can get that off," Nera said.

"I'm not sure I can get it any hotter," he said. Melting iron required a vast amount of magical heat, and he couldn't risk using all of his stores at once.

316

Tapping a finger against the metal, he decided to try a simpler approach. He heated the offending chain only at the links that held it to the fence. Then he pulled against the unheated end, forcing it away from the gate. Grinning, he looked to his companion for approval.

"Do you want me to congratulate you?" she asked, growing impatient. "Just get the third lock open."

The third lock proved no obstacle for Kwil's magic, and sprang open with ease. The gate swung wide, admitting the two intruders to the manor grounds. They crept inside, closing the gate behind them and moving off to the side in hopes of avoiding detection.

"That was almost too easy," Nera commented, her eyes darting back and forth.

The pair remained crouched as they moved along the perimeter of the fence. Kwil knew not to try entering through the front door. No noble in his right mind would allow a stranger to waltz inside, especially one who had just disabled the locks on his front gate.

"Let's go around the side," Kwil said, pointing to an open window.

Nera nodded and led the way, but a sudden movement ahead stopped her. Placing an arm in his path, she blocked Kwil from going any farther. Eyes shone in the fading light, wild eyes. "Those don't look friendly," she cautioned.

Ahead of the intruders paced a dozen large, doglike creatures. They had shaggy fur and hunched backs, their front legs longer than the back. Their yellow eyes gleamed, their white fangs shimmering in the moonlight.

"What are they?" Kwil asked.

Nera shook her head. "I've never seen a creature like that. Maybe it's some hybrid wolf they use for protection."

As she finished her sentence, one of the beasts caught her scent, lifting its nose in the air. A low growl erupted from its throat, its pack mates coming to its side. Kwil immediately summoned flames, which danced in the palm of his hand.

"No!" Nera warned. "Everyone in the house will see the fire. Let me handle this."

The massive dogs charged in her direction, their heads held low to the ground. Nera stepped forward, her heart leaping into her throat. Shoving her fears aside, she opened her mouth, a high note piercing the thick summer air. The beasts stopped short, those behind tumbling over the leaders. Nera continued the song, lowering her pitch. As if in a trance, the dogs lay down, their tongues lolling out of their mouths.

Kwil approached with caution, examining the beasts with magic. "How long will they stay asleep?" he asked, amazed at his companion's ability.

Shrugging, she replied, "I don't know. I don't exactly have a lot of experience with this spell."

"Then we'd better hurry," Kwil said. A high-pitched shriek sounded from the distance, and Kwil's Gatan ears turned toward it. "Did you hear that?" he asked.

"I did," she replied with a nod. "It came from over there." Pointing toward the back of the property, where the faint light of torches illuminated figures in the distance. "I bet you anything that's where they keep the slaves." Another cry echoed, filling her mind with images of torture.

Kwil glanced at the open window and then back toward the screams, his mind torn between two options. He had come all this way for the medallion, but he couldn't ignore the suffering taking place under his very nose.

Nera placed a hand on his arm. "I'm going over there," she said, her green eyes sincere. "If you have any chance at getting that medallion without facing

Arsden, you'll be better off alone. Two of us will make too much noise."

"Your route could be more dangerous than mine," he replied, the words sticking in his throat. Who knows what lengths a sorcerer might go to in order to keep his slaves protected from thieves?

"I'll be careful," she promised. "We came for the medallion, so go and get it. I'll take care of those people. If there's a way to free them, I'll find it."

Kwil had never seen Nera so confident. Though new to her magical abilities, she had stopped the dogs with barely any effort. Her eyes spoke louder than her words. "Don't take any unnecessary risks," he said. "Try to avoid any Gatans."

With a grin, she replied, "Hey, I know what I'm doing." Patting him on the back, she added, "Good luck to you."

"I'll meet you down there," he said, pointing to the slave area. He watched in silence as Nera trotted away in the darkness.

Kwil stepped over the sleeping guard dogs as he made his way to the open window. No need for spells this time. A nearby crate gave him the height he needed to pull himself inside. The room was completely dark, his Gatan eyes taking only a moment to adjust. It appeared to be an unused bedroom, as there were no dressings on the bed and no logs in the fireplace. *Nera was right,* he thought. *Getting inside is proving too easy.* The fur raised on the back of his neck, his senses heightening to the slightest sound. Caution was warranted here.

Cracking the door open, he peered out into the corridor. A human slave carrying a tray walked only steps away, turning down another hallway. As the footsteps faded away, Kwil crept out, sticking close to the wall. Regretting that he hadn't removed his boots, he cast green magic over his feet, quieting his steps as he moved along. *Where would Arsden keep the medallion?* he wondered. Remembering that the other nobles he had worked for always kept their most valuable possessions in their private chambers, he decided to look there first. The lord of the manor would not have his room on the ground floor. Kwil moved steadily along the hallway, peering down each adjoining corridor until he spotted a staircase.

As he tiptoed down the hall, another human slave crossed his path. Freezing in place, Kwil observed her, briefly catching a glimpse of the woman's face. Her eyes appeared white, as if she were enchanted. *I suppose that's how a master wizard keeps his slaves in line,* he thought, a hatred burning in his chest. This man was a true monster. He traded in human lives as if they were lower than insects. Not only that, Arsden had wronged Kwil's mistress. More than ever, Kwil hoped to face the master wizard and exact punishment for his many crimes. But was he truly ready?

Taking a deep breath, Kwil tried to remain calm. After reaching the staircase, he cast a spell over the wood, hoping to prevent any creaking as he climbed. The stairs were wide, and turned sharply before spilling out onto the second floor.

Another slave walked away from Kwil, his movements stiff and unnatural. The mage searched his mind, wondering what spell might break these people from their enchantment, but in his heart he knew the truth. The spell could be lifted only by the master who placed it upon them. Arsden would have to be coerced into removing the enchantment. The only other way to break the spell would be to kill him. Kwil stared momentarily at his hands, wondering if he could take the life of another being. Despite Arsden being a slave breeder, Kwil wasn't sure he could go so far. Such acts could lead down a dark road, and he wasn't prepared to travel it.

Silently moving along the corridor, Kwil scanned the doors, wondering which one might lead to Arsden's chambers. A strong sense of magic emitted from the door nearest him, and he wondered if the medallion held magical powers. If so, it might be what he was sensing. Gathering his courage, he placed a hand on the knob and turned it, gently pushing open the door. Darkness greeted him inside, and he breathed easier believing the room to be empty.

A flash of light erupted in the fireplace, stopping the young mage before he could take another step. Light flooded the room, the figure of a Gatan in a hooded robe sat near the fire. He was older, distinguished, with a stark white coat and blue eyes. Without an introduction, Kwil knew who he was facing. It was Arsden. The magic he sensed was coming from him, a spell of protection surrounding him.

"I sensed your magic when you broke my locks," Arsden said, coming to his feet. "I allowed you to continue out of sheer curiosity. What could bring a young sorcerer to my home?" Crossing his arms, he stared at Kwil expectantly.

"I've come on behalf of my mistress," Kwil replied, his chin jutting forward. "You have wronged her, and

I intend to make it right." He spoke loud to hear his own voice over the pounding of his heart.

Arsden laughed. "And who is your mistress?" he asked.

"Seela," Kwil replied.

The wizard's eyes focused on Kwil, the smile disappearing from his face. "Seela," he repeated. "She should have been left in the woods to die as an infant, but her mother insisted on waiting until she was old enough to have a fighting chance."

"You stole her inheritance," Kwil said, taking a step forward.

"And why shouldn't it be mine?" Arsden replied. "After all, I was the one who arranged the accident."

Kwil cocked his head to the side.

"I see she hasn't told you everything," Arsden said with a chuckle. "I killed her parents, or at least, I arranged their deaths." After a pause, he added, "Perhaps she didn't know."

Kwil felt the blood rising to his face. An image of Seela in her loving mother's arms flashed in his mind. This man had taken everything Seela held dear. He had to be punished.

"Of course," Arsden continued, "arranging such a simple accident was almost beneath someone of my talents, but it was a means to an end."

Not wanting to hear any more of the sorcerer's words, Kwil struck. Summoning the flames inside his body, he fashioned a fireball in the palm of his hand. Launching it in the sorcerer's direction, Kwil could only watch as it bounced away from his shield, returning to the one who had cast it. His Gatan reflexes on alert, Kwil flattened himself against the floor, allowing the fire to pass by him, striking the wall instead. Arsden raised a hand to douse the flames, and then turned his anger on the intruder.

Kwil tried to regain his footing, but he felt as if a hand were holding him against the ground. Rolling over, he felt a second hand pressing against his throat. Panic set in, his lessons of clearing his mind momentarily forgotten. Seela's voice echoed in his ears. *Concentrate!* Despite his lack of oxygen, Kwil managed to steady his mind. Closing his eyes, he visualized the hands lifting away from him. He pushed with all his might to repel them, every muscle in his body tensing.

Arsden took a step back as his spell was broken, the silver-furred Gatan clamoring to his feet. Flames danced in the young man's palms, but Arsden had decades more experience. Summoning a gust of wind, he knocked Kwil backward, sending him tumbling end over end until he crashed against a wooden chair.

His head reeling, Kwil found his way onto his knees, his sights locked on the master wizard. A shimmering blue light emitted from Arsden's hand, heading straight for Kwil. Without hesitation, the young man shielded himself with red energy, the master's magic striking it with great force. Crying out in pain, Kwil barely managed to maintain the shield.

Why did I come here? Kwil wondered, pouring all his energy into his shield. *I'm so stupid to think I could do this. I'm just a slave.* Tears came to his eyes as he realized he had failed his mistress, and might not survive long enough to tell her. *Maybe humans weren't meant to practice magic*, he decided, hanging his head. *How could I ever be a match for a Gatan master?* The thought gave Kwil pause. It was his Gatan form that was draining his magical stores. Maintaining the façade was taking up resources he needed for the fight. Dropping the spell, he instantly transformed into a human, an exhilarating burst of magic running through his veins.

Arsden lobbed another attack, this one absorbed by the young man. Kwil rose to his feet, his resolve strengthening. Arsden threw spell after spell, turning to all four elements, but Kwil absorbed them all, restoring himself to full strength.

"Impossible!" Arsden shouted, his face red with anger. "Humans can't perform such magic!" Not only were his magical stores dwindling, his pride was injured. This was no Gatan who had come into his home. This was a mere human, a creature unworthy of the dirt on a Gatan foot. With his options quickly running out, Arsden focused his remaining magic into his shield.

Kwil approached at a steady pace, his hands glowing with red magic. Unleashing a barrage of flame, he pummeled the master sorcerer's shield, weakening it until it burst in a shower of red sparks. Arsden raised a hand to protect himself, but his magic had run out. The young man had absorbed every drop.

"You should have practiced more," Kwil said with a grin. His opponent was finished, and he, a mere human, had bested a master Gatan wizard. With one hand, Kwil locked his opponent in place, forcing him to the ground. In his other hand, he summoned fire, but the spell was not intended to burn. Instead, it formed itself into a rectangle, spreading over the master wizard's body.

"What are you doing?" Arsden shouted, lifting his hands to touch the magic. He felt a solid wall of heat surrounding him, encasing him with fire magic.

"Release the slaves from their enchantment!" Kwil demanded.

"I will not," Arsden spat.

"Then you will rot in this prison," Kwil threatened.

Fuming with rage, Arsden demanded, "Release me!"

"Your prison will unlock when you've freed those slaves," Kwil replied. As he spoke, a feeling came over him that he had not expected. An image of the enchanted slaves passed through his mind, and his magical stores tingled. When he placed Arsden under his own command, Kwil had gained power over the slaves as well. Squeezing his eyes shut, he focused his magic toward the slaves. *You are free,* he projected with his mind. He could feel them responding, their own free will returning to them. Turning back to Arsden, he said, "It looks like I didn't need you for that after all." With a smile of triumph, he released white magic over Arsden's immobilized form.

The master wizard could not resist, his eyes sliding closed as he looked upon Kwil's smiling face. He fell into a fitful sleep, his mind full of hate.

Kwil's eyes scanned the room, searching for any chest or coffer that might hold Arsden's jewelry. There, on the mantle, stood a small golden box, and Kwil knew he had found the treasure he sought. Opening the delicate container, he pushed aside a ruby ring and a sapphire necklace. A single medallion of silver lay at the bottom, his mistress's energy radiating from it. Gently lifting it from its resting place, Kwil clutched it in his hand. He had done it. His mistress would be pleased.

Tucking the medallion away in his pocket, he hurried down the stairs and out the front door. There was another task to be done.

Chapter 24

Nera stepped softly as she made her way to the rear of the manor. Remaining in a low crouch, she hoped to avoid any eyes that might be searching for intruders. It was unlikely the dogs were the only guards in this area.

Before her spread a series of pits dug deep into the ground. A few of them lit with torchlight, she could clearly see humans inside. As she moved closer, she could see some of the figures were pacing, all of them chained by either wrists or ankles. Another cry caught her attention, the scream of a woman in agony. Scanning her surroundings, Nera proceeded toward the source of the cry.

Only a few yards ahead, two guards dressed in leather armor strode heavily across her path, forcing her to flatten herself against the ground. She held her breath as they passed by, neither taking any notice of her as she lay still in the darkness. Turning her head, she saw other sets of guards, all in pairs, pacing along the edges of the pits.

Another scream from the woman forced Nera back to her feet, her leg muscles complaining about the crouched position. Regardless of the pain, she had to stay low and keep her movements slow and steady. Otherwise, she risked discovery and severe punishment.

Ahead in the darkness, she could see three torches burning in a small wooden structure. Inside was the sobbing of a woman and the rattling of a chain. Nera's heart leapt to her throat, her ears tingling as she listened for any clue to how many guards might be inside. She heard only one muffled voice, aside from the woman.

Approaching the structure with caution, Nera knelt low and brought her face close to the wooden slats. With one eye, she could see between the boards, the image playing out before her of a Gatan towering over a chained human woman. The Gatan drew back his hand, striking the woman across her face. She did not cry out, instead hanging her head and remaining silent.

She had no strength left to react. Swaying a moment, the woman toppled over onto the dirt floor.

The Gatan proceeded to kick the woman, and Nera could no longer sit still. Taking to her feet, she charged inside, not caring whether she was seen.

"Who the—" the man started to say. He never finished his question. Nera grabbed the torch nearest the open door and swung, slamming it against the side of his head. He dropped to the ground unmoving. The human woman scrambled to her knees, her eyes wide.

"Don't worry," Nera said. "I've come to help you." She searched the man's unconscious body for a key but found none. "Where do they keep the keys to your shackles?" she asked.

The woman shook her head, tears flowing from her eyes. "I don't know," she whispered.

Nera looked around the room but saw nothing that would be helpful. "I'll find the key or I'll find an axe," she said. Pausing before she walked out, she said, "I'll be back for you."

Outside it appeared none of the guards had heard anything. They paced as they had before, lazily strolling from pit to pit. Choosing the pit farthest from any guards, Nera broke into a run. A man sat inside, gnawing away at a crust of bread. Startled by Nera's sudden appearance, he dropped the bread, and retreated to one side.

"I'm here to help," she said. "Do you know which guard has the keys?"

The man stuttered a moment, then said, "In the tower." He pointed to a tall structure at the farthest end of the pits. "He's always there, leaning on the rail and twirling them on his finger." He spat on the ground. "He'll be armed," he cautioned.

"So will I," Nera replied, her voice confident. Leaning against the side of the manor, Nera spotted her weapon. It was only a spade, probably used by slaves to dig their own pits, but it had been forgotten and left in the open. *Idiot guards,* Nera thought. One of the slaves could have grabbed it and taken out his revenge. Instead, it awaited Nera's arrival, its wooden handle sturdy, its iron blade dull but heavy enough to do serious damage. Grabbing the weapon, she checked the position of the guards before proceeding toward the tower.

Keeping a close eye on the tower window, Nera crept closer to its base. She saw no one looking out. Silently she ascended the winding staircase, holding the spade against her chest. As she climbed higher, her foot encountered something abrasive, likely sand or pebbles, her footsteps no longer silent. Each breath came more rapidly, but still she continued despite the scuffling sound on the floor above her. Then, a figure stepped out in front of her, a blade held at the ready in its hand.

"Who goes there?" a male voice asked.

Nera did not reply. Instead, she clutched tightly at the spade, readying herself for a fight. The man moved down a few steps, his eyes taking in the intruder.

"A woman?" he asked, surprised. He lowered his dagger slightly.

Nera saw her opportunity and didn't hesitate. She brought the spade up, connecting its handle with the man's face. He cried out in pain and staggered to a lower step. Nera walked past him and turned, bringing the spade down against his back. The guard shouted and tumbled roughly to the bottom of the stairs. Nera raced down after him, turning his limp form over to search for the keys. Attached to his belt was an iron ring with four keys. She took notice of the blood on the man's head, but he appeared to be breathing. Feeling little sympathy, she yanked the keys from his belt and headed back to the slave she had spoken to.

"I got them," she called to him in a low voice.

The man looked up at her in surprise. Raising his wrists toward her, he allowed her to unlock the shackles. Beneath the metal, his skin was red and raw. He rubbed at them slightly and said, "Thank you."

Removing one of the keys from the ring, she handed it to the slave. "Go and free as many of the others as you can," she said.

The man nodded and took the key before creeping toward the nearest pit. Nera ran back to the wooden building where she had left the woman. The guard was still unconscious, and the woman had not been moved.

Kneeling next to her, Nera unlocked her shackles. "Can you walk?" she asked.

The woman nodded and rose slowly to her feet. Her gait was unsteady, but Nera did not have time to carry her.

"Stay close to the others," Nera said. "I'm getting you all out of here."

Stepping outside the building, Nera's eyes immediately caught sight of a scuffle in the pits. Two of the guards had been alerted and descended on the unshackled slaves. From the corner of her eye, Nera saw the man she had freed. He was still unlocking slaves, avoiding the guards entirely. *Good,* she thought. *The more we have free, the more that can fight these guards.*

Lifting her spade, Nera charged toward the guards, striking one on the side of his head. He crumpled into a heap, the slave he had been fighting unable to believe his eyes. His face was covered in fresh cuts, but he ignored the pain, leaping at the second guard. Nera lifted her spade again, but another slave jumped in to help, blocking her chance for a clean blow. Together the slaves pummeled the guard until he dropped, then quickly scampered out of the pit.

"There are dogs too," the injured slave warned.

"I already took care of them," Nera replied. She removed another key from the ring and passed it to him. "Unlock anyone who isn't yet free," she said. Looking around, she realized there were over a hundred human slaves here, and it might take longer to release them than she had thought.

The first man returned after unlocking nearly thirty slaves. "There are more guards coming," he shouted. "The noise has surely woken them by now."

"Then we have to unlock as many humans as we can so they can join the fight," she replied.

With a nod, the man ran off to continue his mission. Nera stopped a passing slave and handed her the final key. "Free everyone you can find," she said.

Not far from her position, Nera saw a blast of red light. In the sudden flash, she could just make out Kwil's form. He was fighting the guards as well, throwing fire at the men as they exited the guards' quarters. Sighing in relief, Nera could not be more grateful. There would be no battle. Kwil had set the guards' beds ablaze, sending them running into the night.

Running toward the source of the flames, Nera shouted, "It's good to see you!"

"I got the medallion," Kwil said quickly. "I see you've taken care of everything here."

"Almost," she replied. "There are still more slaves to unlock."

Hurrying to the farthest pits, Nera proceeded to use her key, while Kwil focused on magic to unlock more slaves. A shout nearby alerted him to the presence of two more guards, but he summoned the flames and threw it their direction. The two men scattered, narrowly avoiding the fire. Losing courage, they ran in the opposite direction, their better judgment telling them not to fight a sorcerer.

The first slave reappeared, searching for Nera in the chaos. "My lady," he said. "I've sent the others to the property's edge. Where do we go from here?"

"I'm not sure," Nera admitted. "And you can call me Nera."

The man gave a nod. "You may call me Dael."

"When Kwil returns, we'll ask him what to do next," Nera said. Her eyes searched the immediate vicinity for her friend, spotting him near the edge of a pit.

Kwil finished freeing what he believed to be the last person before scanning the area with magic. He visualized each pit, checking for any signs of life. He saw no movement. The fire raged on at the nearby guards' quarters, but all of the men inside had fled. There was no one left, save the few people still inside the manor.

Satisfied that everyone had made it to safety, Kwil returned to Nera. The human male at her side gave him pause. He stared intently into the man's eyes as he slowly approached. "I know you," he said, the magic inside him flickering to life.

The man shook his head. "I don't believe we've met," he said, wrinkling his brow. He had spent years in the pits, and many had come and gone, but Kwil's face was unfamiliar in the dark surroundings.

Kwil summoned fire in his hand and brought it near his face. "What about now?" he asked.

Dael took a step backward, his sight fixated on the young man before him. Kwil's face was familiar. It was his own, at least in his younger years. "It can't be," he whispered. "Kwil."

"It is," Kwil replied, stepping toward the man. He embraced him as if he had known him forever.

"Does someone want to explain it to me?" Nera asked, her hands on her hips.

Turning to his friend, Kwil gave her a soft smile. "This man is my father," he said.

Nera examined Dael's face more closely. "You look similar for sure," she commented. "But how can you be certain?"

With a slight laugh, Kwil replied, "Magic."

Dael made no effort to hide his tears. "In one night I find not only freedom, but my son," he said. "Your mother will be pleased to see you."

"You know where she is?" Kwil asked. "Tell me." This was a moment from his dreams. Not only had he found the father he never knew, but the mother who visited his dreams was also alive and well somewhere.

"She wasn't the same after they took you from her," Dael explained. "She no longer resigned herself to this life as I had. She managed to break free and is a leader among our kind. She works with sympathetic Gatans, ferrying our people to freedom."

"You know of this, but you haven't joined her?" Kwil couldn't believe his father would choose to stay behind willingly.

"I had not the courage to follow," he admitted, lowering his gaze. "But seeing my own child so brave, I have found new courage this night."

"I want to meet this mother of yours," Nera said to Kwil. "I'm sure you do as well. We could work with her to end this evil practice once and for all."

Kwil nodded. "I want that more than anything."

"First we have to get this lot to safety," Nera said, indicating the gathered humans.

"Where will we go?" Dael asked.

Considering a moment, Kwil responded, "To Master Rili."

A broad grin spread across Nera's face. "He's going to love having this group swarm by."

"They can't all go at once," Kwil replied. "They'll draw far too much attention."

341

"And we'll be easy to track," Dael pointed out. "A group this size isn't going to traverse the forests without leaving signs of their passage."

"Yes, they can," Kwil replied. "I can cast a spell over all of you, masking your movements."

"You're full of surprises aren't you, Son?" Dael beamed with pride.

"He's studying to be a master wizard," Nera announced. "But all that aside, I think it's time we get moving. Reinforcements are bound to show up sooner or later."

"Good point," Kwil replied. "Let's get moving."

Joining the freed slaves, Nera, Kwil, and Dael led them into the wilderness surrounding Arsden's property. Pausing a moment, Kwil used magic to draw a detailed map in the dirt to Rili's manor.

"You should go to him alone, Father," Kwil said. "Tell him I sent you and follow his instructions on how to proceed." He had every confidence that Rili's conscience wouldn't allow him to turn the freed slaves away. Rili had connections, and he would know the best way to conceal everyone until they could get to safety.

"Come with me," Dael said. "There is so much I want to learn about you."

Though his heart yearned to follow, Kwil could not. "I have to return to my mistress," Kwil said. He owed her that much, and he wasn't ready to halt his lessons. "But we'll meet again soon. I promise."

Dael grabbed his son and squeezed him tightly. "I can never thank you enough," he said. "Or you," he added, looking at Nera.

"Get these people to safety," Nera replied. "That's thanks enough for me."

Dael nodded and sucked in a gulp of air. He stood taller and prouder than he ever had before. "I will," he replied.

Nera and Kwil watched as the group moved out of sight, disappearing among the trees. Their work had only just begun, but a hundred lives had been saved this night.

Running his fingers over the medallion in his pocket, Kwil said, "I think it's time we found Dirnda and got out of here."

"Agreed," Nera said.

Keeping to the edge of Arsden's property, they made their way back to the gate. The sun was on its way up, bringing a pale pink light along the horizon. The first birds of morning began to chirp, their movements visible high in the tress. Dirnda, however, was nowhere to be seen.

Chapter 25

"I don't like the odds of getting back to Seela without Dirnda's help," Kwil said, his eyes scanning the woods. Without the puca's speed to aid them, there was a good chance of encountering resistance along the way. If Arsden's fleeing guards had raised the alarm, Kwil and Nera might have a fight on their hands. It was likely an army of reinforcements were already heading toward the manor.

"I'll take care of it," Nera said. "He made us a promise, and I intend to see he keeps it." Placing her fingers in her mouth, she gave a loud whistle. Staring expectantly into the distance, she awaited Dirnda's arrival.

"Maybe you should try again," Kwil said. "It doesn't look like he heard you." He was quickly losing hope. Dirnda was much too fast for the guards to have done him any harm. It was more likely the puca decided not to wait all night for the pair to return.

Taking in a deep breath, Nera dug deep into her small magical store. Closing her eyes, she lifted her voice, a deep alto note flowing from her lips. Quiet at first, her song became louder, echoing from the trees that stood in the distance.

Kwil caught sight of a shape moving toward them, two glowing orange eyes appearing in the dim morning light. To his amazement, Nera had managed to use the Cry a second time in less than twelve hours. "I thought Seela said the Cry could be used only every few days," he commented.

Shrugging, Nera replied, "Maybe she underestimated me." Nera couldn't explain it herself. All she knew was she needed to use the magic, and it was there for her, though it varied slightly from the one she'd first learned.

Dirnda made his way toward them as if in a trance. Looking upon Nera, he said, "You bewitched me." Dipping his head slightly, he added, "I think I quite like that." He gave a mischievous laugh and motioned with his head for the two to climb aboard.

The pair obeyed, Nera taking the front seat this time. With the thunder of hooves, Dirnda sprinted through the forest at top speed as the sun continued its ascent. The countryside passed by in a haze of green beneath a pink sky, the forest eventually swallowing the trio as they journeyed on. The familiar sight of the Dark Forest lifted Kwil's heart as he anticipated returning the medallion to its rightful owner.

Dirnda paused only steps from Seela's door, allowing the pair to climb down. He stamped at the earth, eager to continue his long run.

"You could come inside if you like," Kwil said.

"After you change form," Nera added.

Dirnda whinnied and shook his head. "I have other things to tend to today. Give my best to Seela." With those words he turned and galloped away, his long tail swishing behind him.

Kwil rushed inside, finding Seela curled up with a book. "Mistress," he said. "I've brought a gift for you." He could barely contain his excitement as he retrieved the medallion from his pocket. He dangled it from its chain before her, his heart full of love and devotion.

Seela's golden eyes drank in the shiny object before her. Lifting a paw, she gently touched the silver surface

347

before clutching it in her paw. "I don't believe it," she whispered, still staring at the medallion. Engraved on its surface was an image of the sun, the symbol of her mother's house. Her eyes wet with tears, she asked, "How did you find this?"

"I paid Arsden a visit," he replied.

Narrowing her eyes, Seela asked, "He gave this to you?"

Kwil glanced at Nera before saying, "Not exactly."

"You fought him, didn't you?" Seela asked, her tone dry and flat. How could this young man have been so reckless?

"I did, Mistress," Kwil replied.

"You went along with this?" Seela asked, looking at Nera.

"I did," she replied.

"I can't believe the two of you would risk your lives for this," Seela said. "You could have been killed. Both of you!" Her tone quickly changed to a mixture of anger and disbelief.

"I had to right the wrong that was done to you, even if only in a small way," Kwil replied. "I can't give you your true birthright, but I can give you this." He dropped to his knees. "Please, Mistress. Don't be angry." He had expected her to be elated, not upset.

Nera placed a hand gently on Kwil's shoulder. "He did it because he loves you," she said. "And I helped because I love you both. Kwil knew he wouldn't fail."

"I would never have let you put your lives at risk for this," Seela replied, her tone softening. With love in her eyes, she looked at each of them and said, "My sweet children." With her arms spread wide, she grabbed Kwil first and hugged him tightly, a purr escaping her throat. She hugged Nera as well, giving the girl a kiss on her cheek. "This means the world to me," she stared down at the medallion, her tears splashing on its surface.

"You've given me so much," Kwil said. "I'm pleased to be able to give you something in return."

"But how did you manage it?" she asked. Kwil was still in training. He wasn't prepared to fight a master wizard.

"Dirnda gave us a ride," he began. "And Nera helped get us past the guard dogs. After that I climbed in a window and met Arsden face to face. I guess he was out of practice." He grinned, not wanting to exaggerate what had happened. He had nearly failed, and he would make sure to go in much more prepared the next time there was a master sorcerer to bring down.

"Did you kill him?" Seela asked, concerned not for her uncle, but for Kwil. She knew he would bear the scar always if he took another being's life.

"I left him alive," Kwil replied.

Seela closed her eyes, nodding in relief. "And you, Nera, where were you during all this?"

"I went through the grounds and released the slaves," she replied.

Chuckling, Seela said, "You make it sound so simple. The two of you have accomplished something amazing."

"All in a day's work," Kwil said, trying to downplay the previous night's events.

"No," Seela said. "If you can best a master wizard, then you have no further need of my instruction."

"What are you saying?" Kwil asked, his breath escaping.

With a wistful expression, Seela said, "There is no more I can teach you that you cannot learn on your own. Your greatest work lies ahead of you. You will transform the land of Gi'gata, but you can't do it sitting here with me. It's time you left the nest and went in search of your destiny."

"But I haven't mastered fire magic!" he protested. How could she send him away? Why didn't she want to continue as his teacher?

Seela patted his arm, her golden eyes softening. "You are mastering Ancient magic, which is inborn and no less powerful than elemental magic. One doesn't need to master an element to be a master sorcerer. You're well on your way to that. I couldn't be more proud of you."

Her words brought him some measure of comfort, but he still wasn't ready to leave. "I want to stay with you," he said. "There is so much I need to learn. I can't do it alone."

"I'm not going anywhere," Seela reassured him. "We can study together as equals whenever you are ready to return. For now, it is time you learn awhile on your own."

"How long must I stay away?" he asked.

"That is up to you," she replied. "Take however long you need. I'm not sending you away, I'm giving you a push toward greatness. This is the best thing for you. The world will teach you things that I can't."

Kwil could see the wisdom in her words, but he wanted to stay by her side. She was more a mother to him than anyone had ever been, and he wasn't ready to break that connection. "What if I return tomorrow?" he asked.

"Then I will welcome you with open arms," she replied with a sigh. "But I hope you will take advantage of this opportunity. Nera is anxious to get going."

"She's right," Nera said. "I love it here, but I can't find a troupe in the forest, and I don't see any slaves that need freeing. I have to leave if I'm going to do those things."

Kwil's heart sank. He was losing Seela and Nera at the same time. It was almost too much to bear. "I can't believe you're leaving too," he said.

"Yes," Nera replied. "I'm going with you."

His eyes wide, he asked, "You are?"

"Of course she is," Seela said. "You two are destined for great things, but only together. I think I told you that already."

Kwil grabbed Nera and hugged her. Suddenly the thought of leaving didn't seem so dreadful. "We won't be gone long," he promised Seela. "Someone has to answer all my questions while I figure out what it is exactly that I'm supposed to do."

"I'm always here for you," Seela replied. Disappearing upstairs, she returned moments later with a black robe. "This is yours," she said, presenting the robe to Kwil. "I had it tailored for you and enchanted it myself. It will change color as needed."

Stroking the soft fabric, Kwil said, "It's wonderful. Thank you." The pair embraced again.

"Now get out of here," Seela said, giving him a gentle push.

Nera ran upstairs to retrieve her lute, leaving most of her belongings behind. Knowing Kwil, it wouldn't be long before they visited again.

Kwil retrieved a few items, including a handful of books he intended to read. "I'll see you again soon," he promised.

"I look forward to it," Seela replied.

Side by side, Nera and Kwil headed out into the forest, both anxious to see what the world had in store for them. Nera hummed a cheerful tune, warming her friend's heart and reassuring him that all would be well. Little conversation passed between them as they journeyed along, eventually emerging from the woods and re-entering civilization.

Stepping forward, Kwil looked down the road and into the past. A young slave boy in rags stood before him, the hope in his eyes undiminished by his years of servitude. Now he was a sorcerer, mastering his craft. No longer bound by chains, he was free to choose his own destiny—to make his own way with his friend by his side.

About the Author

Lana Axe lives in the Missouri countryside surrounded by dogs, cats, birds, and reptiles. She spends most of her free time daydreaming about elves, magic, and faraway lands.

For more information, please visit: lana-axe.com.